The Confession

of

Tobias Tucker

Book Two of the *Lethal Legacy* Series

Sherri Stone

This book is a work of fiction. Names, characters, places, and incidents are the product of the author's imagination and are used fictitiously. Any resemblance to actual events, locales, or persons, living or dead, is coincidental.

Big, big thanks to…

~ Sharon Hinks, from Fiction Fix-It, my editor. I believe finding you was a God thing. Thank you for fixing my work, praying for me, teaching me, and through it all, making me laugh.

~ Rachel Rollyson, for your time and attention to detail, and the many corrections and suggestions. I don't know where you found the time, but I'm grateful.

~ Mom and Dad, for your proof-reading. I could have used you just now when I actually wrote 'poof' reading.

~ Travis, from ProBookCovers.com for the amazing cover.

~ Everyone who has asked about this book and waited anxiously for it. I get a warm fuzzy every time I hear about that. I hope you will love it. Thank you for your support.

~ Jeff.   You are my special gift from God. I like to think I'm his special gift to you. Doesn't he have an amazing sense of humor? Thanks for talking me down off the ledge and for fixing things. I love you very much. You're my favorite.

Mom and Dad: Fiction writers learn to "show don't tell." It makes the story more powerful. That is true in fiction and in life. All our lives you have shown us how to love Jesus and serve him by the way you have loved and served us and others. There is no greater legacy parents can leave for their children. If I can live up to even a small part of that, I will be grateful. I love you. Sherri

Chapter One

My Dearest Grace,

It will no doubt seem strange to hear from me after a lifetime of silence. I am getting older and feel that my time may be short, and I do not wish to meet my maker with this terrible secret on my conscience. It is long past time for us to meet and I have many regrets, not the least of which is never being part of your life. It was your father's wish and seemed right all those years ago, but now I find myself wishing for that time back and for the chance to do things differently. I have followed your life and career with great pride and I believe you are the one who will redeem the family name. I write today to ask a great favor of you and humbly ask you to consider my request, presumptuous as it may seem. I need your help to set right a forty-year-old wrong. I have been a coward, and because of that good people have suffered. I need your help, though I have no right to ask. Please come to me, Grace. Once I tell you the whole story I hope you will agree to help me, but if you choose not to I will, of course, understand and respect your wishes.

I hope we can meet soon. It is the one thing that gives me hope.

With deepest affection,

Tobias Tucker

Grace Tucker stared at the letter in her hand, the slight flutter of the paper mimicking the tremors inside her. Tobias Tucker. The paternal grandfather she had never met. His name had rarely been spoken in their home while she was growing up and to this day she had no idea what had caused such a rift between her father and his family.

A torrent of emotions flooded her - anticipation of finally learning the truth, yet fear of the same. Underneath it all, suspicion closed ranks around her heart. Why her? Why now? What did her grandfather think she could possibly do about something that happened forty years ago, something of which she had no knowledge?

She dropped the letter on the kitchen counter and grabbed a bottle of water from the fridge, taking long drinks, focusing on the cool water and the simple act of swallowing-anything normal. It didn't do much to restore her equilibrium. She picked up her phone and dialed.

Please let her be there.

"Hey, Grace, what's up?" Dani's calm, alto voice floated to her and Grace took her first full breath in what felt like days.

"I need a girls' night out."

A pause. "Okay. You all right?"

"Yes. No. I don't know. I need to talk. Can we meet for dinner?"

"Just say when."

"Mexican. Thirty minutes. Can you call Lucy?"

"Consider it done, sweetie. Are you okay to drive?"

"I'm fine. I'll see you soon." She retrieved the letter and slipped it into her purse. Keys, jacket, out the door. It was time for some serious girl talk.

* * *

Grace arrived first and was shown to their usual girls'-night-out table. Just sitting in that familiar spot began to center her again. A waiter walked by with a tray of margaritas and Grace tracked him across the restaurant. She blew out a breath, picked up her menu, then put it down again. She didn't need it - or the margarita. She stopped drinking after college and had never missed it. Until tonight. Right at this moment she could have used a drink, a sure sign she shouldn't have one.

The waiter delivered chips, salsa, cheese dip, and drinks as Dani and Lucy slid into the booth with her. They ordered their usual and Lucy leaned in to hug Grace. "What's up honey?"

"I got a letter from my grandfather today."

Dani dunked a chip in melted cheese. "I've never heard you mention your grandfather."

"Me either." Lucy sipped her Coke and went after another chip. "Where does he live?"

"He lives in Highgrove, near the coast. I've never met him."

Two sets of eyebrows raised, chips halted - briefly - en route to open mouths.

"Wow. Okay. So, I take it the letter was a surprise?" Dani resumed eating but kept her eyes on Grace.

"Totally."

"And not a good one?"

"I don't know. I guess I haven't decided yet."

The waiter brought their meals and Grace pulled the letter from her purse and handed it to Dani. "Here. Read it for yourself, then tell me what I'm supposed to think."

Dani read and passed it to Lucy then sat back with her tea. "What's he talking about?"

Grace shook her head. "That's the million-dollar question, isn't it? I have no idea."

Dani frowned. "I know you said you'd never met him, but didn't your dad ever talk about him?"

"Never. I know something happened when my dad was very young and it was bad enough to split the family. He left home as soon as he could join the army and never went back. He severed all ties with my

8

grandparents and the rest of the family. I never knew why, and we never talked about it."

"Not ever?" Lucy talked about everything. Grace knew she couldn't comprehend having such a family secret, and doubted if anyone could stand up very long against Lucy's interrogations.

"Nope. Never. I don't even think my mother knew the whole story." Grace played with her spoon. "It was kind of a lonely way to grow up. We moved a lot because of the army and we didn't even have family to visit when he was gone."

"A forty-year-old wrong. That sounds so mysterious." Dani's eyes sparkled with interest. "I can't imagine no one ever spilling the beans in all this time."

Lucy looked at the letter again. "Do you think he was dangerous or maybe abusive?"

Dani tapped her finger on the table, lips pursed in concentration. "I don't think it's about him."

"Why do you say that?"

"Well, for one thing, he's asking for help to make things right."

"Trying to clear his conscience."

"Yes, but read this line again. *I have been a coward and because of that good people have suffered.* It sounds more like something he covered up than something he actually did himself. He knew something. He should have spoken up but he didn't. Now he wants to come clean."

"Okay. Maybe. But what are we talking about?" Lucy asked. "Someone stole the silver, or maybe someone's wife? Or something worse?"

Grace pressed a hand to her stomach and pushed her plate away, her appetite as elusive as the answers she needed. "Who knows?" she said, angry at her father's determination to keep the family secret.

Just like his father did.

"I wish I'd never gotten this letter."

Their waiter came to clear the table and Dani ordered dessert.

"Could we have a fried ice cream, please? Just one, with three spoons."

Grace's stomach churned in protest.

"The real question is," Dani continued, "what are you going to do about it?"

"I don't know. That's why you two are here."

"You want us to tell you what to do?"

Lucy snorted. "That'd be a first."

"I'm asking for suggestions. I'm not promising to do what you say."

Lucy looked smug. "That's what I thought."

Grace blew out a breath and ran her hands through her hair. "What if I just don't go?"

"What if you don't?" Dani threw the question back at her. "Do you spend the rest of your life worrying about what you might have fixed, or wishing you knew the secret?"

Grace shrugged. "I don't know. I've wondered about it almost my whole life so you'd think I'd be jumping at the chance to find out."

"Exactly. So why aren't you? What's changed now? If it were me I don't think I could stay away." Lucy's curiosity knew no bounds.

Grace sat back and picked apart her napkin. "I used to think it was only a misunderstanding that just blew out of proportion. Not such a big deal. But now…" She glanced up at Dani and Lucy. "I'm afraid it's something much worse. He said he was a coward. My father kept quiet about it too; does that make him a coward? And what if I decide not to go? Am I continuing the family tradition?"

Grace grabbed a spoon and dipped into the fried ice cream with more force than was necessary. If she couldn't have a margarita she could at least have ice cream and chocolate syrup. She licked her spoon and closed her eyes, savoring the moment. "It makes my stomach hurt."

"The ice cream or the enchilada?" Lucy asked.

Grace rolled her eyes. "The grandfather thing."

"Let's say you do go." Dani rested her arms on the table and leaned toward Grace. "You need some way to assess the situation, to be sure you'll be safe. He gave you his phone number. Why don't you start with a phone call? It's not perfect, but you can tell a lot about a person from one conversation. If you get a bad feeling, don't go. He said he'd respect your wishes. Hold him to it."

Grace nodded thoughtfully. "What if I don't get a bad feeling? What if I like him?"

"You probably will like him." Lucy grinned. "You like everyone. I've never seen anyone with the ability to find something good in people like you do."

"This is different."

"Yep." Dani looked her straight in the eye. "This is personal. Very personal. And…"

Grace resisted the impulse to squirm under Dani's sharp stare. "And?"

"And the consequences-no matter what decision you make-will be personal as well." Dani reached over and tapped Grace's arm lightly. "You need to think through this, Grace. It's highly likely you'll be hearing some hard things. Are you ready to deal with your father's silence? Are you ready to be associated with whatever the family secret is? Knowing comes with some responsibility. What if this is a secret that needs to be told? Will you be able to do that?"

Grace closed her eyes and tried to breathe. *I wish I hadn't eaten.*

"We haven't helped much have we, sweetie?"

Grace opened her eyes to see Lucy's worried face and had to smile. "Of course you have. I didn't expect you to fix it for me - well, I wouldn't have minded that. I'm just glad you came. I needed some perspective."

The waiter returned with the bill. Grace reached for it but Lucy got to it first. "My treat tonight."

"Take some time to think about this," Dani said. "You don't have to make a decision tonight. Think through each choice to the logical conclusion and decide what you need to do from there. Whatever you decide, we're with you."

"Absolutely," Lucy chimed in. "We just want you to be happy, Grace. And safe. Please be safe."

* * *

A week later, Grace curled up in her over-sized recliner with the letter in her lap as she brushed out her freshly washed hair. The mindless task helped to soothe her. The herbal scent of her shampoo was light and comforting and combined with the warmth of her hot tea to relax her.

Since dinner with the girls, she had thought of little else besides the letter and what her response should be. The whole situation triggered a sadness she had not anticipated. She missed her mother all the time, but never as fiercely as she did right now. Ellen Tucker had always been her sounding board, her advice gentle and wise. Grace had no doubt that if her mother were here now she would know exactly the right thing to do. She would talk to her, not keep a secret that was hurting her.

But her mother didn't know the secret. Her father had never confided in his own wife. That both angered and scared Grace. Why would he leave them in the dark about something so important? And how bad was the secret that her father had to take it to his grave?

She sighed. In a perfect world, she never would have received this letter. No, in a perfect world there would have been no terrible secret. No wrong to be made right. In a perfect world, she would have grown up knowing her grandfather instead of wondering what kind of man he was.

She had only one choice, really, if she ever wanted to have peace. She took a deep breath and reached for her phone. It was time to meet her grandfather.

Chapter Two

Quaint. That was Grace's first impression as she drove into the town of Highgrove. The two-lane highway bisected the town and the park in the center of the town square, each side a mirror image of the other with small, hometown businesses lining the streets. Children played in the park and everyone obeyed the fifteen mile-an-hour speed limit. Grace punched the button to let down her window and breathed in the scent of freshly cut grass, one of her favorite memories from childhood. A smile tugged at the corners of her mouth to be quickly chased away by thoughts of why she had come. This beautiful little town – only two hours from her home – held an ugly secret and somehow her family was right in the middle of it. Like the Stepfords – pretty and perfect on the outside, not so much behind closed doors.

Her grandfather had given nothing away during their phone call. Their conversation had been awkwardly polite, mostly because she had no idea what to call him. Mr. Tucker felt too formal, but she wasn't ready for Grandfather or any of the possible permutations of that title. That would have implied a relationship that didn't exist. They settled on Tobias. She had accepted an olive branch, such as it was, but wanted the option of leaving if needed, with no emotional ties.

Probably too late for that, Grace.

Eight miles east of the pretty town square Grace turned onto the long, gravel driveway that led to her grandfather's home and rolled to a stop. Dogwoods in full pink and white bloom lined the entire length of the drive connected by hedges of perfectly-shaped, purple azaleas that formed a solid wall of color. Southern Living magazine couldn't have done it better.

She pressed a hand to her chest and blew out a long, slow breath. Beneath her hand, her heart pounded rapidly. Fight or flight? Should she continue up the drive or turn and run back home? She couldn't remember ever being so conflicted.

Not going to get any easier, Grace. Just make a choice and get on with it.

* * *

Tobias Tucker paced before the huge picture window of his study. He stopped every few steps to stare out and frown. The car at the end of the drive had to belong to Grace. People sometimes used his drive to turn around, but no one ever just sat there. What if she changed her mind? So much depended on her.

"Doris!"

"Right here, Tuck. What is it now?" His housekeeper frowned at him as she hurried into the room in response to his bellow – again.

"Where's my coffee?"

"In your coffee cup."

He followed the line of her finger pointing to his desk and the cup that no longer steamed with heat, and scowled.

"It's cold."

"It happens. I'd get you some more but that'd just get cold, too. Staring out that window won't make her get here any faster."

"She's here," he said softly.

She took in a small, quick breath and moved to stand next to him. "What do you think she's doing down there?"

He placed his hand flat against the window. "If she's smart she's deciding to go back home and forget she ever heard from me." Sadness and guilt almost brought him to his knees. "What have I done, Doris?" he whispered. "What in the world have I done?"

Doris linked her arm through his and rested her head on his shoulder. "What you had to do, Tuck. What other choice did you have?"

Tobias watched as the car made its way slowly to the circle drive in front of the house. "I could have done what I've always done," he said, bitterly. "I could have left it all buried in the past. I'm good at that."

A young woman got out of the car, looked around, and headed for the steps that would bring her into their lives, and into the middle of a nightmare.

"Too late to change your mind now, old man," Doris said as she pushed him toward the foyer. "I'll make some fresh coffee. You go say hello to your granddaughter."

* * *

Grace raised her hand to knock but the door swung open and she took a startled step back as her breath caught in her throat. Pictures of a younger version of this man were scattered throughout her home. The hair – dark in the pictures, snowy white on the man before her – was the same thick, unruly mess. The same build. Same posture. But the eyes…that same forest green. Her father's eyes. She had those same eyes.

Do you see my father in me? Do I look like family to you?

A deep sense of loss opened in her like a pit, dark and empty except for the pain and anger stuffed inside. It had been a mistake to come here. She wasn't ready, would never be ready for this. Panic threatened. She had to leave.

"Grace?" Those green eyes clouded with concern under a furrowed brow. "Are you all right?"

She drew in a deep breath to steady herself and nodded. "I'm sorry." Her voice shook and she swallowed hard. "You look so much like him. My father."

He nodded. "It hasn't been so long that I forgot. We always did favor one another. No way to prepare you for that shock, I guess. I'm so glad you came. Please come in."

He stepped back and waved her through the foyer. She stepped in past him and jumped when the door shut behind her.

"I'm sorry," she said as he joined her again. "I can't remember what to call you."

"Tobias, for now," he said. "Maybe one day we'll work our way up to Grandfather. No pressure there, Grace. Like I said on the phone, my only expectation is that you listen to my story. After that, we'll see where things go."

He led her to his study and motioned her to a large, well-padded chair next to a beautiful round table in front of the picture window. Instead of sitting, she walked around the chair to the window to gaze down the drive where she had been parked contemplating this visit and what it meant. Tobias came to stand with her.

"It's a lovely view from here," she said. "You must love working in this room."

"I do. It's a peaceful scene, especially this time of year when the gardens are blooming. I can't think of many things prettier."

Footsteps sounded lightly on the carpeted floor pulling her attention from the window. A woman carried a tray of coffee and cookies to the table.

"Thank you, Doris. I'd like you to meet my granddaughter, Grace Tucker." Tobias motioned Grace around to her chair. "Grace, this is Doris Landon, my housekeeper and the woman who keeps my life running smoothly."

Grace smiled and extended her hand. "Hello, Mrs. Landon. This looks delicious, thank you. I hope you didn't go to any trouble."

"It was my pleasure, and please, call me Doris." Her whole face smiled, her eyes warm and friendly. "I'm so glad you came, Grace. It's a visit long overdue."

Grace looked at Tobias and nodded. "Yes, I think so, too."
"Well, I'll be working on dinner and let you two get acquainted. Just
holler if you need anything." Doris pointed her finger at Tobias like a
mother warning a child. "And you be on your best behavior."

"Yes ma'am." Tobias' eyes twinkled and for a split second his
smile was unguarded and relaxed. He poured coffee for them both and
handed Grace a pretty china cup and saucer. "She's not just my
housekeeper."

Grace added two cubes of sugar. "I got that impression." She
stirred and wrapped her hand around the small cup, absorbing the
comforting warmth.

"Don't go jumping to conclusions now. She's a friend and has
been for a long time. That's all. We've both been alone for a long time
and this arrangement works for both of us. I don't know what I'd do
without her."

Grace gently set her cup down and clasped her hands together in
her lap. "Wasn't it your choice to be alone?"

"Actually, no." He sighed, started to take a sip of coffee, then
carefully set his cup on the table. "Grace, I know we have a great deal to
talk about and I want to tell you everything. Would you mind terribly if
we left that part for tomorrow? I would like you to have some time to get
settled and relax, and for us to get acquainted tonight. Start to, anyway.
Would you agree to that?"

All her mother's training on the importance of being a polite and
gracious guest warred with rising impatience. She tried to measure her
next words carefully. "Tobias, your letter made this visit sound urgent,
like you were running out of time. If you're sick or something…"

"No, no, nothing like that." He waved away the suggestion. "I'm
not getting any younger, but…there are some people who would prefer
to leave things as they are. In some ways, many ways, I guess, it would
be easier all the way around."

"Except for your conscience."

"Yes, except for that." His smile was a sad one. "Conscience can be the very devil." He moved to stand in front of the window, hands clasped behind him. "Grace, I hope you understand that I'm offering more than just an explanation of what happened all those years ago. I'm offering you-well, both of us-a chance to be a family."

Grace stood but didn't join him at the window. "I get that, Tobias, but I think I need to take one thing at a time."

He nodded. "Let's start with dinner, then." He came back around the chair to face her. "I'd like you to stay here during your visit, Grace; that is if you're comfortable doing that. If not, I'll be happy to get you a room in town."

He looked very vulnerable and unsure of himself, and Grace's sympathetic nature made the decision for her. He wasn't any more comfortable with this than she was, maybe less since he had the confessing to do.

"I'll stay tonight, Tobias, thank you, but I can't promise any more than that right now."

"Fair enough," he said, relief evident on his face. "Let's get you settled and we'll have a good talk over dinner."

* * *

Grace stepped into the dining room freshened up but not refreshed. The hour-long should-I-stay-or-should-I-go debate had been an exercise in futility.

Make your case and make it good, Tobias. I'm not in the mood to get jerked around tonight.

Tobias held her chair and a sweet sadness opened inside her.

"My father used to do that," she said softly. "Thank you."

"We taught him to be a gentleman, his mother especially." Tobias chuckled. "He could never pull anything over on her."

Doris came from the kitchen with a basket of freshly baked rolls and a pretty little plate with pats of butter. She declined Grace's offer to help as she poured tea and water.

"You sit right there. I've got this. I'll bring dinner out and leave you two to visit. I'd like to get home before the bottom falls out."

Grace glanced through the lacy curtains. Dark clouds blew closer and in the distance, rain fell in thick sheets, headed straight for them.

Nowhere to run to. Nowhere to hide.

Doris brought plates for them both and Tobias stood.

"I'll walk you out, Doris."

She waved him back to his chair. "No need. You stay and eat while it's hot. I'll be back in the morning."

"She's bossy, that one, but she can cook like nobody's business." He pointed with his fork. "You're going to love her pork roast and gravy."

"It smells delicious." She ran her finger over the delicately embossed handle of her fork. "Tell me about my grandmother. What was she like?"

Pain flicked across his face. He lifted his napkin to the table and meticulously smoothed out the wrinkles. "She was the greatest woman I ever knew. We met in high school and from the moment I first saw her I knew she was the one." He smiled and a twinkle lit his eyes. "Didn't make it easy on me. She made me chase her for a year or better before she let me buy her a coke. It was worth it, though. She was full of life and loved to laugh, and she loved our boy," he finished softly.

"When did she die?"

"Twenty-two years ago, last October. She was sick for a few years before that. Cancer." He took a slow sip of tea. "Some days it feels like she's been gone forever, and others…well, I still start to call her and tell her about something that happened during the day."

"Were she and my father close?"

"Like peas in a pod. She was never the same after he left, like

19

something died inside her. I think…" He shook his head, then fell silent.

Grace pushed her plate away. *I was eight when she died. Did Dad know?*

She frowned. "No matter what had happened, I can't believe he would have missed her funeral."

"He didn't."

It took effort to draw in breath. "What?"

Tobias' eyes blazed with intensity. "He didn't miss her funeral. And I didn't miss his."

She flushed hot, then went icy cold. A hundred questions raced through her brain, not a single one of which managed to make it past her lips before disappearing, leaving her mind a total blank. The silence pulsed with barely contained emotion, ready to explode. She couldn't look away. Anger, pain, and deep sorrow rode waves from Tobias to Grace, like vibrations from a tuning fork headed for delicate crystal. How long before she shattered?

"Tobias…"

He leaned closer, his eyes hot with intensity. "He was my boy, Grace. My only son. Do you think I would have stayed away?" He pushed his chair back and paced. "He wouldn't have wanted me there." He whirled around to point a shaking finger at her. "He had the say all those years, but not then. Not when he died. I left him alone because he asked me to, but he didn't get to keep me away when they buried him." He drew a ragged breath and braced on the back of his chair. "All those wasted years. For what? To protect the family?"

Grace swallowed hard. "Why, Tobias?" Barely a whisper. "Why didn't you let us know you were there? We needed you. Why wouldn't you stay and see us?"

"He made me promise to stay away from you. He didn't want his family touched by any of this. I had to respect his wishes. Can you understand that?"

Grace shook her head slowly. "How can I?"

Tobias sat heavily, as if the weight of the world pushed him down. "I had no right to you. I'd never been part of your life. Daniel was mine. Even when he decided he didn't want to be anymore, he was still mine. I made so many mistakes, but I loved him with everything in me. I couldn't let him go without saying goodbye."

"That was five years ago. What made you break your promise to him?" Grace stared into those pain-filled eyes. "Why did you write to me, Tobias?"

He sat back and studied her for a long moment. "Why did you come?"

I had no choice.

The wounded part of her heart cracked open and the loneliness of the past five years seeped out, and with it the truth of why she'd come.

"You're a part of my father, a connection to him." With effort she steadied her breathing. "I miss him so much," she whispered. "Everything changed when he died."

Tears glistened in his eyes. "I understand. You're my connection to him, too. I disappointed him. No, I made him ashamed of me. I understand why he wanted me to stay away from you. I don't blame him for that." He pulled in a deep breath and straightened his shoulders. "I think he would approve now. I'm choosing to believe that. I'm going to do what I should have done back then. I'd like us to do it together, Grace, as a family. Are you willing to help me before it's too late?"

Well that's the question, isn't it?

Chapter Three

Grace groaned as she sank into the deep soaking tub. A push of a button added jets of air that combined with heat to massage muscles tight with the tension of the past few hours. She rested her head on a pretty neck roll and closed her eyes as the bubbling water and steam lulled her into a relaxed state, somewhere between sleep and awake. When she started to sweat, she ran through a quick shower, then grabbed her phone and sprawled on the bed to call Dani.

"It's about time you called! I've been going crazy wondering what's going on. Tell me everything? How are you? What's he like?"

Grace laughed. Dani was always so…Dani. "I'm fine. Sorry I didn't call sooner, but I think I fell asleep in the hot tub."

"The hot tub. I see."

Grace grinned. "The hot tub. Massaging jets and bubbles. The works. I really needed it."

Dani snorted loudly.

"That's so pretty. Have you done that for Matt yet?" Just hearing Dani's voice made Grace feel lighter.

"I have no intention of doing that for Matt. And don't try to change the subject. Tell me everything. What's the house like? If there's a hot tub in the guest room it must be great. What about Tobias? Please don't make me beg for info."

Grace fluffed the pillows behind her. "Tobias is…nice. Polite. Nervous."

"And?"

"Dani, he looks so much like my father," she whispered.

"Oh, honey I know that must be so hard. Is he like your dad in other ways?"

"I don't really know yet. I was expecting some nice, polite conversation for dinner but…" She proceeded to give Dani a play by play of the evening. It was just as exhausting the second time around. "After that I just couldn't wait to get to my room." She grimaced. "That sounds really bad, doesn't it?"

"Not at all. I'm in total awe of you going there at all. I just wish you hadn't gone alone."

"I think I needed to. Besides, I think he's going to have enough trouble spilling his guts to me without having an audience." A pause. "I think he has a girlfriend."

She could almost see Dani coming to attention.

"I know you're not going to drop that bombshell and stop there."

Grace sighed theatrically. "If you must know, her name is Doris and he says she's the housekeeper."

"Do tell."

"Uh huh. He made a special point of saying that they're just friends. They've both been alone a long time—"

"Well whose fault is that?"

Grace grinned. "We're talking about that tomorrow. Anyway, she's been working here since before my grandmother died, about forty years. She doesn't talk to him like he's her employer and he doesn't seem to mind that at all. Oh, and she's a great cook."

"Hmm."

"What?"

"Hmm? Oh, nothing, just thinking."

"About?"

"It's nothing."

"Dani—"

"Okay, I was just thinking about the timing, you know-forty years? It's probably nothing, but isn't that about the time your father

23

split from the family?

Grace sat up slowly as the sense of well-being from the bath and conversation slipped away. *How did I miss that?* She rubbed at her forehead trying to get to the ache homesteading there. *Maybe it's just a coincidence.* It could happen. She had liked Doris from the beginning and her instincts were almost always spot on. *Am I just completely off base here?*

"Grace? Gracie, are you okay? I'm sorry sweetie, I didn't mean to upset you. I was just thinking out loud, which I shouldn't do."

Grace inhaled slowly. "I'm fine. I just never made the connection until you said something. I don't know where my head is."

"I'm sure it's just a coincidence. Just weird, that's all."

"Maybe. Housekeepers always know the family secrets. I don't know why this should be any different."

Doris would be protective of Tobias, that much was clear. Maybe they were close because of that. Would her presence make it easier for Tobias to talk or harder? Grace slid off the bed and padded across the room to dig in her purse for ibuprofen. She popped three with some water and turned off the lights as she returned to the bed. She desperately needed sleep. Tomorrow promised to be a long and trying day.

"Okay, enough of this for tonight," Grace said. "Tell me about Matt. You two have been getting pretty serious, haven't you?"

She was relieved when Dani allowed the subject to be changed without a fight. Dani would understand that Grace needed a break, and lately she was always ready to talk about Matt.

* * *

Grace woke slowly, pulled from a dream where someone was hammering. She tried to hang on to the vision but the pounding distracted her. She opened her eyes and looked at the clock on the bedside table. Eight-thirty. She rolled to her back and groaned. Now the pounding came from her bedroom door. Someone was knocking, loudly.

"Who is it?"

"It's Doris, Grace. I've brought you some breakfast. May I come in?"

Grace pushed herself up, shoved hair away from her face and tucked the covers around her. "Sure. Please come in."

The door opened and Doris entered with a tray delicately balanced in one hand. "Good morning." She smiled as she set the tray on the bed beside Grace. "I thought you might want to take your time this morning. Tuck and I always eat early."

"Is he waiting for me? I can get dressed first."

"He's gone into town for some supplies and to take care of a few things, so you don't need to hurry."

Grace frowned, her frustration at yet another stall making it difficult to keep suspicion at bay. "I'm getting the feeling he's avoiding this conversation."

Doris motioned to a chair. "May I?"

"Sure, I'm sorry, please sit down. And thank you for breakfast, my manners are usually better than this. You really didn't have to go to any trouble."

"It's no trouble at all." She smoothed down her skirt with both hands. "Be patient with him, Grace. He's nervous about you being here. Oh, I don't mean he doesn't want you here. He does, and that's why this matters so much to him. He wants to get it right, and he's afraid you won't stay. I haven't seen him this way since…"

"Forty years ago?" She locked eyes with Doris. "You know everything, don't you, Doris? You could tell me the secret as well as Tobias could, couldn't you?"

Doris stood and poured tea for Dani, refusing to make eye contact. "I'll let you finish your breakfast in peace," she said as she headed out the door. "Tuck will be home in about an hour and he'll want to take you on a tour of the property. It's beautiful this time of year."

Grace took a long, slow breath to try to quell the queasiness that settled like a rock in her belly. So much for allies. She tried to tell herself that avoiding the question wasn't the same as lying but she couldn't stop the feeling of disappointment that enveloped her as Doris quietly left the room.

She flopped back down on the bed and stared at the ceiling. One hour. She would be dressed and ready when her grandfather got home, and she would get some answers. If he kept stalling, she would leave. She didn't owe him anything.

Chapter Four

Doris warned him that Grace was getting antsy. No, she was getting tired of the stalling. It wasn't helping him either. How in the world would he find the words to explain it, and to someone who wouldn't see the story in context? He would look like a monster. Maybe he was a monster. He didn't know anymore.

So many regrets. He'd tried to make things better all those many years ago. Hadn't he protected the family? With one notable exception.

He entered the kitchen as Grace came through the back door from the garden. "Good morning, Grace. Did you sleep well?"

She nodded as she filled a mug with coffee. "I did. I think the hot tub had something to do with that."

He smiled. "One of the best decisions we made when we built this house." He filled his own mug. "Thank you for your patience, Grace. I guess there's no time like the present. Shall we have a talk?"

She nodded. "I think it's time."

He led the way back to his study and took a seat across from her. She curled up with a pillow clutched tightly in front of her, and stayed silent while he gathered his thoughts.

"Do you know much about the family history, Grace?"

She shook her head. "Nothing really. Mom didn't know anything and Dad never talked about it. I know he was sad sometimes. Mom said it was the only secret he ever kept from her. Even when he knew he was dying, he still didn't say anything."

"The family history in this county goes back six generations, all the way back to the eighteen hundreds. My great-grandfather came here from Ohio and bought land as he could afford it, started a business and raised a family. We've always been involved in local politics, serving on city councils and the like. Grandfather felt it was important to give back to the community. He was raised in a generation that still believed you left a place better than when you found it. Every generation since then has tried to live up to that. And we always have." He paused to sip his coffee.

"Until something went wrong," Grace said softly. "Or someone."

"Yes." He wasn't sure he could get the words out. The coffee in his cup shimmied with the tremors in his hands, and he put it down before it sloshed over the side. He tried to take a deep breath but anxiety gripped his lungs like a fist, allowing just enough air to stay alive, but no more. His heartbeat pounded in his ears and he could hear little else.

"Just say it, Tobias." Grace pushed her hands through her hair. "It'll be easier on both of us if you just get it over with."

She was right. He glanced past her shoulder out the window and recognized the car kicking up dust as it moved down the drive. The Sheriff, who was young enough to be his grandson, was in a hurry. That did not bode well for Tobias or the conversation, which would now have to wait. He was both relieved and profoundly disappointed. He didn't know how many times he had it in him to do this. He glanced back at Grace. She would be angry, and he didn't blame her. He just hoped this didn't send her packing.

* * *

She wanted to scream in frustration. When the doorbell rang, Tobias fled the room. What in the world was Doris here for if not to answer the door and run interference for him when he didn't need to be disturbed?

He's about to be disturbed. He's about to be the victim of

28

serious bodily injury if he keeps putting me off.

She heard voices in the hallway and followed the sound to the foyer. Tobias and a young man in uniform talked in hushed tones. The stranger's uniform consisted of well-worn jeans, a button-down shirt, and a cap with the initials CCSO embroidered on the front. Cullen County Sheriff's Office. A badge on his chest and a gun on his hip completed the look, one she might have taken the time to appreciate if she hadn't been so angry.

Both men noticed her at the same time, and conversation ceased. She suddenly felt like an intruder which sparked her temper.

Tobias's smile was tight and strained. He held out his hand to her, motioning her closer. "Grace, this is Zach Wells, our Sheriff. Zach, Grace Tucker, my granddaughter."

The sheriff gave her a long, appraising look from head to toe, as if sizing up someone he'd been hearing about. His smile was as strained as Tobias', but he extended his hand. "Pleasure, Ms. Tucker. I hope you'll enjoy your visit here."

Right.

A lifetime of training kicked in. Grace shook his hand. It was warm, strong, and calloused. The hand of a working man. "Thank you, Sheriff, and it's Grace."

He nodded. "Zach." He didn't wait for a response before turning back to Tobias. "I know it's a bad time, Tuck, but Henry needs to see you right away. Says it's urgent. I'll be glad to drive you over if you'd like?"

Tobias managed to look both apologetic and relieved as he spoke. "Grace, I'm sorry. I know this is not a good time for another interruption but it can't be helped. We'll finish our talk as soon as I get back. I promise." He turned to Zach. "I'll meet you at the car in a minute, Zach."

Zach glanced between Tobias and Grace, then pulled out his sunglasses and nodded. "I'll be waiting. Nice to meet you, Grace. I'm sure I'll see you again soon."

When he was gone, Tobias grabbed her hand and held it tightly. "Grace, things may get a little tense around here for a while. It's nothing for you to worry about, I just need you to trust me a little while longer."

I don't trust you now.

She shook her head and frowned. "What does that mean, Tobias? Does this have to do with why I'm here?"

He looked at his watch and glanced out the door. "I'll explain everything as soon as I can. I promise."

Grace moved to block him when he headed for the door. "I'm sorry but you've been saying that since I got here. Maybe I should just go home and come back when it's…"

That stopped him cold. "Grace, please. I can only imagine…please wait for me. If we don't get to finish our conversation today I promise I'll help you load your car so you can go home." He squeezed her hand tightly. "Just a little more time. Please say you'll stay."

"I'm not staying another night, Tobias. I'll wait, but then I'm leaving."

His shoulders sagged with relief. "Okay. Okay. That's fair. Thank you, Grace. I'll be back soon."

She stepped to the side and he headed for the waiting car. The anger drained from her, to be replaced with something much more unsettling.

Maybe I should have said goodbye.

Chapter Five

Zach kept his eyes on the road as he drove north to his grandfather's home. Tobias had been silent since they left the house. "I feel like I interrupted something important back there, Tuck."

Tobias sighed. "You did. We've been trying to have a talk since she got here yesterday. Things keep coming up." He grimaced. "She's losing patience. You have any idea what Henry wants? I'm real tempted to tell him he'll just have to wait."

Zach glanced over, one eyebrow raised. He'd known Tuck his whole life. He'd played on the floor in Henry's study while Henry and Tuck talked business or politics or played chess. He'd heard them argue and debate and he'd seen them take different sides on important issues, but he'd never heard either one of them sound like they didn't have time for the other. That was new, and it unsettled him in a way he couldn't quite identify.

"Just said it was important and he needed to talk to you before you did something you'd be sorry for. Him too." He glanced at Tobias. "Sounds like you'd know more than me."

He waited for a response but got none. He pulled into the driveway and Tobias stopped him before he could get out.

"I can find my way by myself. You get back to work."

Zack frowned. That wasn't like Tobias, even on a bad day. "You two gonna be okay?"

"Why wouldn't we be? Now go on. Henry and I have some business to discuss. And Zach?"

"Yeah?"

"Thanks for the ride."

Zach watched Tobias make his way to the front door and shook his head. They were both acting weird today. Henry had nearly taken his head off this morning and Tobias was as surly as he'd ever seen him. Whatever it was, he hoped they'd get it out of their systems this afternoon so things could get back to normal.

* * *

Tobias walked in without knocking, the privilege of more than fifty years of friendship. He made his way through the unusually quiet house to Henry's study in the back. It was a man's room, all dark wood with the stuffed remains of animals hanging on all four walls. Henry liked to shoot things.

Tobias had never been able to bring himself to use a gun. Not even when he... He stopped that train of thought. He would be going there soon enough with Grace. He didn't have the stamina to do it twice.

"'Bout time." Henry's big voice boomed, filling the cavernous space of his study. "I sent the boy for you over an hour ago." He paused to light his pipe. "What the devil took you so long?"

Tobias sighed and sank into a chair. "I have company, Henry. I couldn't just run out without an explanation."

Henry eyed him sharply. "How much of an explanation did you give her? You *are* talking about Grace?"

"She doesn't know anything. Yet."

"You still planning to tell her?"

"I am. She deserves to know."

"Why?" Henry had not taken his gaze off Tobias.

"Because, Henry, it's her family, and it's family business."

"It's not just her family, Tuck," Henry snapped. "Or have you forgotten?"

"I haven't forgotten anything!" Anger shot Tobias to his feet where he paced the boundaries of the room, too agitated to sit still. "I've lived with it every day of my life for forty years. I'll die with the shame of it." He stopped in front of Henry's desk to point a finger at his friend. "No, Henry, I haven't forgotten. I wish I could forget. Maybe then I could face myself in the mirror without seeing a bloody coward." He started pacing again. "Do you have any idea what it's like to be ashamed to talk to your own grandchild? Afraid of seeing the look on her face when she realizes what you've done?"

"Then don't tell her."

"I don't intend to die with this on my conscience, Henry. You might be willing to, but I'm not."

"Have you considered the consequences of this, Tuck? All of them?"

Tobias sank back into his chair. *Here it comes.* Would he come right out and say it? "You mean other than my granddaughter hating me?"

Henry's eyes flashed and Tobias knew he'd struck a nerve.

"I mean are you ready for the whole world to know what your family is responsible for?"

A deep sadness filled him. They were two old pit bulls who'd lived under a kind of unspoken truce and who, now threatened, were about to turn on one another.

"And what you've covered up all these years?"

Threatening to expose a man's secrets was risky business any way you looked at it. Henry's face darkened, his eyes hardened and he leaned toward Tobias.

"Do you have any idea what this will do to my reputation? To my family's reputation? For the love of all that's holy, Tuck, what about Zach? He's like your own grandson. They'll take his badge and run him out of town on a rail." He left his chair to pace. "And for what?" he shouted. "Just so you can die with a clear conscience? Why don't you think about someone besides yourself for a minute?"

"Henry—"

"No! You think about this, Tobias. Think long and hard before you do anything. Besides you, who is this going to help? No one. Just you. Is it still worth it?" He planted himself in front of the window, his back to Tobias.

Tobias stood with a weary sigh. "Henry, I—"

The sharp sound of glass cracking stopped him. Henry fell backwards, landing at Tobias' feet. Time slowed, but not the pool of blood spreading under Henry's head. Tobias stared into the open, empty eyes of his lifelong friend. Horrified and enraged, he whirled around to the window and came face to face with the gun that had ended Henry's life, now pointed at the center of his own chest. What shocked him even more was the face sneering at him behind the gun. In that one moment he realized two things. First, the forty-year-old secret hadn't been a secret from everyone. And second, he wasn't going to live to set things right.

Chapter Six

Grace found Doris in the kitchen preparing to assemble a chocolate fourteen-layer cake. That she had no interest in one of her favorite desserts was a measure of her frustration and building anxiety. She casually walked to the counter by the sink, snagged a mug from the dish rack and filled it with coffee, all without saying a word.

She leaned back against the counter and sipped her coffee as she watched Doris. The capable hands that ran her grandfather's home and life trembled slightly. Grace took note and squelched a spurt of sympathy. Normally she didn't like making people uncomfortable. Today she would make an exception.

Doris looked up and tried to smile. "You and Tuck taking a break?"

Grace sipped. "Henry Wells has summoned. You must have noticed that Tobias left. Apparently no one ever says no to Henry."

Doris paled, and dropped her gaze to her piping bag. "They've been friends for years."

"About forty? That seems to be the magic number."

Grace didn't miss the tiny gasp. Oh yeah, Doris knew everything. Grace kept sipping. "I guess it's going to be up to you, Doris."

"I'm sorry?"

Grace moved around the island to perch on a stool. She placed her mug on the counter and traced the rim with her middle finger. Doris's gaze flicked back and forth between Grace and the cake. "You'll have to tell me everything."

Doris stopped what she was doing and stared at Grace, then glanced toward the doorway, looking for an escape.

"Tobias keeps promising we'll talk but things keep coming up, so..."

Doris shook her head. "I can't. It's not my secr—"

The doorbell sounded, and Doris sagged in relief. She dropped her spatula and headed for the door.

Seriously?! It's like they're planning this. She's not getting away that easy.

Grace slid off the seat and followed Doris, arriving just as she opened the door. Zach Wells was back. Only four hours ago he and Tobias had driven away and left Grace fuming with frustration. Now he was back. Alone.

He pulled off his cap and pushed his fingers through his hair. Fingers that trembled. Grace frowned. She had not pegged him as someone who rattled easily. Only one thing she could think of would cause such a reaction. Tobias and Henry.

Grace pushed past Doris and stepped right up to Zach. Even standing one step below her on the porch he was several inches taller. "Tobias?"

He looked at her with eyes full of pain and something else. Fury? She felt the jolt in her gut. "Come inside." She stepped back and he entered and stood looking around as if seeing the place for the first time. He finally looked at Doris.

"Let's go sit down a minute, Doris." He gently took Doris's arm and led her to the study. Grace followed. No one sat.

"Something's happened to Tobias, hasn't it?" Grace moved closer to Doris who looked pale, her eyes wide with fear of what was coming. "Just tell us."

Once again Zach faced Doris as he spoke. "I'm so sorry, Doris. Tuck is dead." He dropped into a chair and braced his arms on his thighs, head bowed.

Doris made a small sound of distress and Grace helped her to a seat, then took one herself. This could not be happening. "He just left four hours ago. With you. He was going to see your grandfather. Where did—"

"Henry's dead, too."

Grace sank back into the couch as her breath left her in a rush. "Zach! I'm so sorry. I don't understand. What hap—"

"Someone shot them – both of them – in Henry's study." He stood and moved to the window. "It must have happened right after I left."

Grace fought the storm of emotions whipping through her soul. There was anger, pain, disbelief, but underlying it all was an overwhelming sense of loss and regret. She had hoped one day to call Tobias grandfather. She had hoped to learn to love him, and to have time to get to know him. Twenty-four hours ago she had not yet met him. Four hours ago he had been very much alive and making her crazy. Now he was gone. Just like that. Murdered. A chill snaked up the length of her spine. Suspicion slithered through her brain and she knew in the depths of her soul that Tobias had been murdered because he was about to tell the secret.

Next to her, on the couch, Doris raised her hands in front of her in question then dropped them back to her lap. "Why? Who in the world would want to kill him?"

Grace faced them both. "Someone who wanted him to keep quiet."

Doris paled even more. Zach turned from the window, jaw set, eyes narrowed and locked on her.

"What do you know about this?"

"I know nothing about this. In fact, I think I should be asking the two of you that same question."

Doris gasped and managed to look both horrified and hurt. Zach simply raised an eyebrow as if daring her to continue.

Well, let's not disappoint!

"Tobias called me here because of something that happened in this town forty years ago, something that was apparently so horrible that no one wants to speak of it. He certainly didn't. He took every opportunity to postpone telling me." She looked squarely at Zach. "Including leaving with you today."

"What are you trying to say Ms. Tucker." He stood facing her, arms crossed over his chest and feet planted wide.

She met his gaze and held it, refusing to flinch from his hard stare. "I'm saying that Tobias's secret got him killed."

They stared at one another for a long moment.

"I don't know anything about that," he said quietly.

Grace rolled her eyes and snorted in disbelief. "Right." She turned to walk away but Zach stopped her with a hand on her arm. She looked at his hand, then up at him.

He dropped his hand. "I know something happened a long time ago but it was just a story to me, old town lore."

"Doris knows."

Zach crouched down right in front of Doris, forcing her to see him. "I need to find out who did this. If you know anything—"

Doris jumped up and Zach was forced to move or get knocked to the floor. She stood wringing her hands as she glared at Grace, accusing. "She keeps harping about the family secret. Family. I don't think spending one day in Tobias' house gives her the right to say she's family!" She looked back at Zach. "If you'll excuse me, I have a funeral to start planning. When can I claim the body?"

"When the medical examiner is finished with the…when he's finished. I'll let you know. I'm really sorry, Doris."

Her whole body seemed to sag with the weight of her grief. "I know, honey. I'm sorry about Henry, too. They were good men."

Doris left. Zach stared out the window and Grace felt like an intruder in her grandfather's home. It wasn't a contest, but she was angry that her grief would never be counted as deeply as Zach's and Doris's. Somehow hers wouldn't matter. Like Doris said, one day in this house didn't give her the right…

Totally at a loss, she sank into an overstuffed chair and studied Zach. He had not moved a muscle, just stared out the window as if willing his grandfather to come down the drive. She pressed a hand to her chest, trying to force back the sadness.

"I'm so sorry about your grandfather, Sheriff. Whatever else is going on here, I can tell you were very close."

Zach dropped into a chair and rested his head against the back. He stared at the ceiling for a long moment before he answered. "My father died when I was fourteen. Henry's been like a father to me since then, even before that, really."

"Do you know what happened? It just seems so incredible that someone wanted to hurt both of them."

"Kill, Ms. Tucker. Someone killed them."

Grace took a breath and nodded. "I got that, Sheriff, I'm just wondering why?"

He leaned forward and looked her dead in the eye. "I thought maybe you could shed some light on that."

She frowned. "What do you mean?"

"Don't you think it's quite a coincidence that you arrive in town one day and the next day Tobias is killed? Aren't you worried he hasn't even had time to update his will yet?"

Molten fury shot through her, launching her to her feet. "You think I killed him? For money?" Hot tears spilled down her cheeks. She wanted to smash something, preferably his face. It would be worth whatever jail time she faced for assault on an officer.

"Look at it from my point of view."

She whirled to face him and took some satisfaction when he held both hands up and took a step back.

"You're new in town, to all of us. Tuck invites you here to tell you some dark family secret. Then the day after you get here someone kills him. And Henry." He shrugged. "It all revolves around you."

"If I were going to kill him, which I didn't – and wouldn't – why would I do it *before* he told me anything?"

Zach rubbed the back of his neck and tilted his head from one side to the other. "I'm not saying you're responsible. I only meant that whatever Tuck was planning involved you somehow."

Grace shoved aside her temper for a moment and tried to remember that whatever else he was, Zach was the grandson of a man who had been murdered a few short hours ago, a man he loved dearly. Grief was not mitigated because you carried a badge. Still, the direction of the conversation and his thoughts unnerved her.

"Have you considered that this is not related to me at all? Your grandfather and Tobias were friends for a long time, from what I gather. I'm sure they've been involved in dozens of business deals over the years, maybe hundreds. This could be related to one of those."

He nodded slowly. "It could be."

"But you don't think so?"

"I...no, I don't." He pulled off his cap and shoved his hand through his hair before replacing it. "I have to go back to Henry's. The state police are handling the investigation. I'm sure they'll want to talk to you."

She had more questions but he was gone. She sank down on the couch, her mind blank. What was she supposed to do now? She didn't know whether to pack up and go home or stay and...and what? She had been willing to help Tobias. Well, at least hear him out. Too bad he hadn't been willing to talk.

Chapter Seven

According to Doris, mornings were Tobias's favorite time of the day. He liked nothing better than to be outside when the air was cool and crisp and the day was new and quiet. He would have loved this day. A slight breeze ruffled grass and women's skirts and tugged at carefully coiffed hair.

The cemetery in the churchyard was mere steps out the door of the small chapel. Grace hung back, uncomfortably aware of the sidelong glances and hushed whispers of the crowd. Once again she felt like an intruder, and was so glad to have Dani and Lucy with her. Doris had not asked her to sit in front where the family would sit. No one knew her, but everyone knew who she was.

Are they all wondering if I killed him? They probably think I'm here just for his money.

The mourners took their places at the graveside and the pastor began to speak. A cloud floated across the sky and stalled in front of the sun as if heaven had dimmed the lights. Grace couldn't tell if the chill was from the air or from inside her. The service was mercifully short. It took longer for everyone to extend their condolences to Doris. *Like she is his widow.* When the crowd had dispersed, Grace caught up with Doris as she was leaving.

"Would you like to ride back to the house with us, Doris?"

Doris shook her head. "I'm not going back. My personal things have already been removed. I'm going to live with my sister."

Grace was stunned. Doris had not said a word about moving out, not in the entire five days since Tobias' death. "Doris, you don't have to do that. It's your home."

"It was only my home while Tuck was alive. I've got nothing there anymore."

"What about the house? What do I do with his things? Who's responsible for taking care of all of that?"

Doris shrugged. "It's not my problem anymore. Do whatever you want. Stay. Go. It doesn't really matter." She hurried off to a waiting car that took her west, away from Tobias' home.

"Wow. Don't go away mad." Lucy stepped up and slung a supportive arm around Grace's shoulders. "She's somethin' else, isn't she?"

Dani stepped up next to Lucy and Grace smiled at them. "Thank you both for coming. I was feeling a bit lost. It's nice to see familiar faces."

Dani looked around. "You mean people who don't suspect you of offing your grandfather?"

Grace sighed. "Yeah, that." She dug her keys out of her purse. "Come on, let's get some lunch before you have to head back."

Dani and Lucy grinned at her.

"What?"

"We're not going back. Not yet, anyway." Lucy looked pleased.

Dani smiled. "We thought you might want some company for a few days so we came prepared. We're your new house guests for the week."

"Seriously?" Relief flooded her. She wasn't alone anymore.

"Yep," Dani answered. "So, do you have food in the house or do we go shopping?"

"It's fully stocked. Doris shopped yesterday." She frowned. "I don't understand her."

"What? Her leaving?"

Grace nodded.

"She never said anything?" Lucy pulled sunglasses from her

purse and stuck them on her face.

"She hasn't said much at all since he died. She's been avoiding me."

"Why would she do that?"

"I pushed her kinda hard. I think she knows what Tobias was going to tell me but she won't talk about it."

They headed for the parking lot as a middle-aged man with silver hair approached and called her name. *Ambulance chaser* flashed through her brain. She resisted the urge to roll her eyes.

"Ms. Tucker, I'm Remington Forsythe," he said as he extended his hand.

Of course you are.

"I'm your grandfather's attorney."

What else could you be with a name like that?

Grace extended her hand and shook his. "What can I do for you, Mr. Forsythe?"

"I'd like to talk to you about Tobias's last wishes. There are some things that need to be finalized."

"I'm not sure how I can help you. I don't know anything about his business."

He smiled.

She shivered.

"I can explain everything you need to know. May I come to the house tomorrow around ten?"

"Uh, sure, ten is fine."

You really need to quit smiling.

"Excellent! I'll see you then." He doffed an imaginary hat. "Ladies."

They all stared as he got into a very expensive car and drove off. Lucy snickered. Dani tipped her own imaginary hat. Grace shook her head trying not to laugh.

"We cannot do this in the cemetery." Lucy's eyes were full of mischief.

Grace looked back across the field to the church. Only a few people remained and they were trying not to look like they were watching Grace and her friends.

"Absolutely," Dani agreed. "Let's go to the house. We can make fun of anyone we want to there." Then one more time... "Ladies."

Grace laughed in spite of herself. She would never have asked them to stay, but she was so glad they were. She wasn't about to argue. "Let's go home."

* * *

Zach watched Grace leave the cemetery with two women who must have been close friends. They acted like sisters. It was the first time he had seen Grace look relaxed. She confused him. When he first heard Tobias had asked her to come, he assumed she would because of his money. No one turned down a chance to inherit.

She was still in his house after almost a week. The state police had questioned her, but were careful about what they shared with him because of his connection to Henry. He didn't get the impression they were focusing on her as a suspect. Yet.

Evidence sent to the lab for processing was caught in a backlog. Though the cause of death was obvious, the state boys would proceed with caution until they had proof in hand. Zach climbed into his official vehicle to head back to the station. Henry's funeral was tomorrow and he had work to do in the meantime.

He let his head rest on the seat and closed his eyes for a moment. The weight of official duties and family obligations settled on him and he had never felt so unequal to the tasks before him. Sleep eluded him at night, but tugged at him during the day. His mind kept going back to Tobias and Henry and whatever had happened all those years ago. He'd said nothing to the state police about that and they operated under the assumption that some business deal Tobias and Henry were involved in had gone bad. It happened.

Zack couldn't let it go. More to the point it wouldn't let him go. The more he replayed his conversation with Grace the more he came to believe that she was right. He swore under his breath. He had some research to do. He started the car and headed into town to the newspaper office, making a quick stop for coffee on the way, and checking in with the dispatcher on duty.

A blast of cold air hit him as he pulled open the door to the local paper. The woman at the desk looked up from her computer and smiled. "Hello, Sheriff."

Zack smiled back. "Hey, Lou Ann. How ya' doin'?"

"Can't complain." The smile faded. "You go to Tuck's funeral?"

"Yeah. It was a nice service."

"As funerals go?"

"Yeah."

"I'll be at Henry's tomorrow."

"I appreciate that, Lou Ann. Henry would, too."

"I still can't believe they're gone."

He nodded. "That makes two of us."

"You think it has anything to do with why Tuck brought that girl here?"

That surprised him. "Why do you ask?"

She shrugged. "You know, people talk."

"Uh huh, and what are people saying?"

A blush spread up from her ample bosom to flood her face. "Oh, you know, the usual gossip." She busied herself straightening a stack of papers that didn't need it.

Zack wasn't falling for it. He leaned over the counter and tilted his head to look her in the eye. "Let's have it, Lou Ann. You hear everything in town."

She stared at him, clearly not wanting to talk. After a moment her gaze dropped to her hands and he smiled. He wasn't above a little coercion, but he didn't want her to feel too bad.

"Lou Ann." He waited for her to look at him again. "You're not in trouble and I'm sorry if I made you nervous. It really would help to know what's being said around town, even if it is gossip."

She brightened. "Well, you know," she waved her hands around in front of her, "some people are wondering about the will and…"

"And who inherits?"

"Well, yeah."

"What else?"

"Um, well I guess a few people are wondering if she killed him for his money."

She was watching him closely for confirmation. He knew it and gave nothing away.

"I see," he said thoughtfully. "And what do you say?"

Her eyes popped wide open. "Me? I don't think anything one way or the other." She made a show of straightening that same stack of papers. "It's none of my business anyway."

In spite of the serious nature of the conversation Zach laughed. "Sugar, everything in town is your business." She frowned and stuck her lip out in a well-practiced pout.

Zach headed around the desk to the stairs. "I'll be down in the archives for a while if you think of anything else."

He didn't have to look at her to see her frown slide into a sly grin. His own smile faded as he flipped on the lights in the musty basement. He'd be back on allergy medication tomorrow. If he couldn't find what he needed down here, he wasn't sure what the next step would be. He could talk to some of the old-timers in town, but he'd rather it not be public knowledge that he was digging up dirt from a generation ago.

He muscled his way past box after box of old newspapers. It was the worst possible way to keep them. The most recent twenty years or so were in large leather-bound volumes that were easy to store and read. Prior to that, the newspaper employees had simply chucked a folded copy of each issue into a box. When the box got full they labeled it and relegated it to the back of the storeroom.

He found a stack of boxes with the dates he needed, pulled them over to the table by the wall and sat down to start searching. *What am I even looking for? This is probably the biggest waste of time...*

He opened the first box and found an assortment of long-dead insects scattered on top of the papers. He carefully lifted the top one out, holding it sideways to allow the bugs to drop back into the box, then replaced the cover. It didn't look like anything alive had been in there for a very long time, but he didn't want any surprises.

Chapter Eight

"I can have any bedroom I want?"

Grace laughed at Lucy as they wandered through the house, as amazed as Grace had been her first day here. "Any one but the middle room on the right. That's mine."

"Do they all have those spa tubs? I could really use some heat and bubbles."

"I don't know, I haven't been in all of them." She smiled at Dani who looked just as impressed. "I'll leave you two to pick your rooms while I scout for some lunch. Just come down as soon as you're settled."

Grace searched through containers in the fridge and settled on the beef stew, dumping it into a pot to reheat. More searching revealed an entire round of cornbread that she wrapped in foil and stuck in the oven on low heat. While she waited for the food, she filled three glasses with ice and poured sweet tea.

She ladled the stew into pretty stoneware bowls, tucked a wedge of cornbread on the side and had everything on the table as Lucy and Dani strolled in. Lucy said the blessing for them and they dug in, slathering real butter on the warm cornbread and dunking it into the delicious stew.

"I'm so glad you guys came," Grace said around a mouthful of stew. "And I'm really glad you're staying for a few days. It's been so weird here."

Dani popped a bite of cornbread into her mouth and licked her fingers. "I'm really sorry about Tobias. That's the most bizarre thing."

Grace nodded. "I know. It still doesn't seem real. I mean, one minute he's here and the next he's dead." She frowned. "I'm sure his murder is somehow related to the big secret."

"But...?"

Grace put her spoon down and sat back. "But, I think the sheriff thinks I'm crazy."

Lucy finished a bite of stew. "This is the sheriff whose grandfather was killed with Tobias?"

"Mm hmm."

"What are the chances that his grandfather and yours were both involved up to their necks?" Lucy hopped up from the kitchen island and dipped more stew. "It makes sense. They'd been friends their whole lives and then they're both killed? In one of their homes?" She punched the air with her finger. "That's not a coincidence."

"No, it's not, and it's creepy," Dani agreed. "The question is, what now?"

Grace pushed her empty bowl away and leaned back. "Not a clue. Any ideas?"

"Not a one." Dani took empty dishes to the sink then leaned against the counter. "Maybe that lawyer will clear things up in the morning."

"Speaking of creepy..." Lucy rolled her eyes and shivered dramatically. "I don't think you should meet with him alone, Grace. I don't trust him. I don't know why, I just don't."

Grace gave her a quick hug as she headed to the sink. "I don't trust him either, honey, and I won't be alone. You two will be right here with me."

That appeased Lucy, and even Dani looked relieved. "Sounds like a plan."

"I've got a better one," Lucy said, and grabbed Dani and Grace by the hands. "Double feature night in the game room." She proceeded to drag them with her to the game room at the back of the house. A theater was set up on one end with floor-to-ceiling shelves on either side of the screen loaded with DVDs. Lucy pawed through the collection. "He's got everything in here. Scary or funny?" she asked, holding up one in each hand.

"Funny," Dani answered without hesitation.

"Funny," Grace echoed. Things were strange and scary enough already.

* * *

Remington Forsythe should have been a seller of used cars. Or snake oil. Or prayer cloths. Grace had not been impressed yesterday at the cemetery. Today wasn't looking so good either.

"Grace. May I call you Grace?" He leaned forward over the table as if to impart some great secret. "May I suggest we speak privately?"

Not unless I'm armed.

"We have some delicate matters to discuss."

With a big can of mace.

"I don't know that you'll want just anyone," he paused to glance knowingly at Dani and Lucy, "hearing the details of your business."

And a gun. A really big gun.

Grace took a calming breath and managed a tight smile. "I appreciate your concern, Mr. Forsythe, but these are my closest friends. They are here at my request. You may speak freely in front of them."

He did not look pleased. He straightened and busied himself with papers. "Very well. Everything must be finalized and signed by the judge, of course, but the long and short of it is this. Tobias made some specific bequests to friends. I will deal with those. He left the bulk of his estate to two charities. One is the local homeless coalition, and the other is an agency that provides support to victims of violent crimes and their families."

Grace nodded and tried to ignore the part of her brain that

screamed those bequests were intended to make up for something. To right the wrongs of the past?

"That sounds like Tobias," she said. "At least from the short time I knew him."

Forsythe tipped his head. "Indeed," he replied crisply.

He bent to his papers again and Grace glanced down the table at her friends. She almost laughed out loud at their expressions. If eye rolling were a competition sport, she'd have the winning team right here. She made a face and rolled her eyes right back at them.

"Your grandfather had three life insurance policies. One will cover his burial expenses. Mrs. Landon has already taken care of that. A second will cover some outstanding debts." He paused and looked up. "As executor of his will I will process those." He flipped the final pages of Tobias' will and scanned as though refreshing his memory.

He pulled an envelope from his portfolio and slid it across the table to Grace. "This is a letter he wrote for you, the day before you arrived, actually. I have no idea what it says. You may read it at your leisure."

Grace carefully placed both hands over the envelope as if guarding a treasure. A letter from Tobias had started this whole thing. Now this letter contained his last words to her. "Thank you," she said softly. "I appreciate you taking the time to bring me this, Mr. Forsythe. I'm sure you're very busy."

"Indeed." He drew out more documents. "I have one more thing, Ms. Tucker. Tobias has left the house and property to you." He ignored the collective gasp from all three women and continued. "In addition, there was one final life insurance policy. He recently updated the policy to reflect a change in beneficiaries, and has named you as the sole receiver of funds." He made a show of scanning the documents as though the information was not indelibly etched on his brain. "This policy is for two million dollars."

Chapter Nine

Zach got to the station early to get in a few hours of work. Henry's funeral was scheduled for two o'clock and he would be gone the rest of the afternoon. He read and signed reports, looked over a budget, perused resumes from officers who wanted to fill the two available spots on his roster, and finished an entire pot of coffee by himself. He needed it. Sleep eluded him and when it came, it was troubled.

He stood and stretched, then made his way to the kitchen to make a new pot of coffee. With any luck, folks would get to the office in time to save him from caffeine overload. Armed with a fresh, steaming mug he returned to his desk.

He clicked open his email and started to scan, deleting several without opening them. He scrolled down until he found the one he'd been waiting for. It was an unofficial ballistics report from the shooting. The state police would get the official report, of course. Technically he shouldn't be anywhere near this case, but he had some well-placed friends who were keeping him informed.

Zach opened that attached report and began to read. Two slugs had been recovered, one from each body. No shell casings had been found at the scene either inside the room or outside where they believed the shooter had been standing. The bullets came from a .380 – a handgun usually owned – and used – by women. They were in good enough shape to be matched to a gun, if one was ever found.

He took a large swig of coffee. The leather chair creaked and groaned as he leaned back, reviewing the information he'd just read. He was trained not to jump to conclusions, to process evidence without prejudice and assumptions. Just because the gun was typically bought and used by women didn't mean that a woman had killed Tobias and Henry.

He knew both men well, but now he questioned that knowledge. His mind raced with unanswered questions and he grabbed a pen and scribbled them down on paper. He flipped the paper over to begin a list of suspects and stopped with his hand poised above the paper, pen ready, mind completely blank. He had no one to suspect. Yet.

The phone rang. "Sheriff Wells."

"Good _orning', Sheriff. You're startin' early today."

The loud, shrill voice made him cringe. "Mornin', Holly. Lots to do today. What can I do for you?"

"Well I've got some news you'll want to hear." She paused for effect. "Remington Forsythe just filed Tuck's will this morning. I got a peek when it was being recorded. It was quite interesting."

Zach leaned forward. She had his attention. Holly was a horrible gossip and the last person who should be working for the court clerk. All kinds of personal and confidential information flowed through that office. Knowledge was power and Holly did like to feel important.

"Hmm?" He didn't want to appear too eager. "How's that?"

"Well, let me just say that I think it's very suspicious, Tuck bringing that woman here to his house."

Zach took a deep breath and prayed for patience. "Well, she is his granddaughter. I don't see anything suspicious about that."

"Well, it just seems to me that a man should do a little checking is all, I mean before he gives away two million dollars to a woman he's just met."

All humor fled as Zach struggled to absorb that bombshell. He was grateful she couldn't see him at the moment and desperately needed to get off the call. "That's a good point, Holly. Listen, I appreciate—"

"Don't you want to know what else he left her?"

"I'm listening."

"Only the house and his land. How much do you think all that's worth?"

He stood now, the adrenaline pumping through his system making it impossible for him to stay in his seat. "Don't have a clue. Listen Holly, I appreciate the information, but I think you need to stay quiet about this until it's supposed to go public."

She sniffed loudly. "It's not like I'm gossipin', for the love of Pete! I'm reportin' something suspicious to the sheriff." She sniffed again. "It's my duty as a good citizen."

"And your sheriff appreciates it. You take care now, Holly, and I sure thank you."

He hung up before she could get going again. The jitters he felt were from the adrenaline rush, at least that's what he told himself as he headed back to the coffee pot for yet another refill. Who needed sleep? Two million dollars. And the house. And the land. A heck of a gift. Not a bad motive for murder either.

He knew nothing about Grace Tucker. Their brief meeting when he'd come for Tuck, and later when he'd delivered the news about the shooting hadn't told him much. He'd interrupted what must have been an important conversation, and she'd made no effort to hide her irritation. She'd been upset and had all but accused him of letting something happen to Tobias. He frowned. Truth be told, he'd been so shocked about Henry he barely remembered getting to Tuck's house and back, much less what her reaction had been.

Zach reached for the phone and dialed the number of his best investigator, Renee Grimes. She answered on the third ring as was her peculiar habit. Always the third ring. Zach didn't mind peculiar as long as it didn't affect her work. In Renee's case, it didn't. She was stellar when it came to tracking down information, so it was worth putting up with a bit of OCD.

"Renee, I need some background on a person of interest."

"Ready to copy, boss. Shoot."

He settled a bit. Renee was as steady and dependable as they came, and he could count on her building a solid picture for him. "I need everything you can find on Grace Tucker."

"Social? DOB?"

"Don't have those, sorry."

"Uh, anything to narrow it down a bit? There's probably several out there."

Zach sighed. He had nothing, which was why he called her. "She's Tuck's granddaughter. Apparently the primary beneficiary of his estate."

"Sounds like someone's been talking to Holly."

"Actually she talked, I listened. It was pretty enlightening stuff." He heard the snort of laughter loud and clear.

"Isn't it always?"

"I know she lives in Union Springs, drives a dark blue Nissan Cube. In her early thirties." He paused. "Does that help?"

"Well it's better than nothing. I'll see what I can do, boss. How soon do you need it?"

"Yesterday."

She heaved a dramatic sigh. "Why do I even ask? You'll have it as soon as I do."

"Thanks, Renee. You're the best."

"I know."

He smiled as he hung up the phone. One thing down. Renee was sassy and cocky, but she always came through. His smile faded as he glanced at the blank piece of paper on his desk. His list of suspects. Most investigations started with those closest to the victim. Since that person was dead too, he would start somewhere else. He grabbed his pen and scrawled the first name on his list: Grace Tucker.

He worked for the next few hours trying not to think about burying the man who had been like a father to him for most of his life.

As if some internal clock kept time, the longer he worked the heavier his heart became. He managed to push aside thoughts of Henry for most of the morning, but now it was time to say a formal goodbye and he had never felt less prepared for anything in his entire life.

His second in command, Ross Taylor, stuck his head in the door as Zach stood and grabbed his coat. "How 'bout a ride, boss?"

"Are you my designated keeper today?"

Ross leaned against the door frame. "It's a thankless job, but someone's gotta do it."

They made it to the church a few minutes ahead of schedule and Zach used the time to spend a few minutes alone with his grandfather. He stood at the casket, still not fully comprehending that Henry was dead. There was no sign of sickness or injury. No reason that big, strong body couldn't get up and go back to work. Those hands had wrangled horses and pulled calves. They'd built fences and worked on equipment. They'd taught him to hunt and fish and had paddled his backside more than once. Those strong arms had held him and comforted him when his father died. *Henry.*

How many times in his career had he stood over a body dreading the next-of-kin notification, never really understanding what it was like to get that kind of news? His thoughts drifted back to his parents, both lost to illness, his mother to cancer, his father to liver disease. Alcohol was a sly poison, and something had driven his father to indulge until it killed him. Those deaths had been hard, but not unexpected, and neither one violent.

This was different. Henry had never been sick a day in his life and should be here now. Zach still couldn't reconcile the fact that he had talked to Henry only a few hours before being called to a crime scene to find him dead. He wasn't prepared. He needed answers. He needed Henry.

He looked up when his uncles, Carter and Wilson, stepped up to the casket. Both looked pale and shocked to see their father. It was the first time he'd seen either of them since he'd told them Henry was dead. Resentment shot through him, the surge so strong he had to turn away and take several deep breaths to keep from venting his anger at them. They'd been less than useless when planning the funeral. Since they'd been that way about most everything as long as Zach could remember, he wasn't surprised. It still amazed him that these weak, overly-sensitive men were Henry's sons.

Carter patted Zach's shoulder in an awkward attempt to comfort him. Zach barely resisted pulling away and kept his eyes on Henry so Carter couldn't see his anger. He deserved Zach's contempt, but now wasn't the time or place. Today was for Henry.

Somehow Zach made it through the two-hour visitation with friends and the community coming to pay their respects. Henry had been an integral part of the community for decades, leaving his mark everywhere. Many were indebted to him in one way or another, and many others had both admired and envied his influence, wealth and power. They all came out to say goodbye.

Zach finished speaking with an older couple and thanked them for coming. He sensed someone step up behind him to the casket and turned, surprised to see Grace Tucker.

"I didn't expect to see you here."

She frowned and looked apologetic, then smiled warily. "I didn't mean to intrude, Sheriff. I just wanted to pay my respects."

"I didn't think you'd ever met Henry."

"No," she said softly, shaking her head. "I never met him, but," her breath hitched a little, "Tobias would have been here. Since he can't be, I came for him."

Zach's steady gaze rested on her for a long moment. "You didn't owe Henry anything, or Tobias, for that matter." He tilted his head, his eyes narrowed and the restraint he'd shown with his uncles completely deserted him. "Maybe this soothes your conscience about that big inheritance you got from Tuck."

She stepped back as if he'd slapped her, eyes wide with shock and cheeks flushed with anger – and hurt.

He'd never wanted to take back words as badly as he did those. He reached out his hand and started to apologize but she pulled away, shaking her head. "I'm sorry. I shouldn't have intruded. Please forgive me."

She all but ran away from him, out the side door. He couldn't go after her. Apologies would have to wait until he fulfilled his obligations here. Guilt piled on top of grief as he turned back to the next person in line and prayed that this day would end soon.

The service ended and he walked behind Henry's casket to the family burial plot in the church cemetery. He'd walked the same path the day before, carrying Tuck's casket. That thought reminded him of his altercation with Grace and he shook his head. He really could be a horse's butt sometimes.

Ross drove him back to the station for his car.

"I'll be available by phone if anyone needs me."

"We'll keep things covered for you, Zach. You need anything?"

"I'm good, thanks. A long, quiet drive and some peace and quiet sound good right now."

Zach trusted Ross to keep things in order while he was gone. He slipped off his uniform jacket and equipment belt and slid into the driver's seat. Country roads were great therapy. Long, not too busy. You could drive for miles on autopilot and just think – or not. He found a CD of Henry's favorite country music and pushed it into the player. Windows rolled down, he headed out on the open road listening to Henry's music and telling himself that the wind in his face was making his eyes water.

Chapter Ten

"I can't believe he actually said that!"

Grace took a quick glance at Lucy's furious face, then focused on the road. It was nice to have friends who got offended on your behalf. Lucy and Dani were both ready to do bodily harm to the sheriff. Instead of sitting at the house plotting felonies, Grace suggested they take a look at the land she had inherited. Tobias owned a jeep and they piled in and enjoyed the ride, between spurts of righteous indignation.

"I know he's grieving." She grinned when both friends snorted in derision. "But he really was a horse's butt."

"How did he know about the inheritance? You just found out this morning."

"Yeah, well, he's the sheriff. I don't think much happens in this town without him knowing."

"And," Lucy chimed in, "a two-million-dollar inheritance is not an easy secret to keep in a small town."

Conversation halted when Grace topped a small rise overlooking a pristine lake. Late afternoon sun glittered on the surface and a slight breeze made continuous, tiny ripples that chased one another from one side of the lake to the other.

"Oh, how beautiful!" Grace turned off the engine so the only sounds were of gently lapping waves, and leaves rustling in the breeze. "I had no idea this was here."

"Wow!" Dani leaned over the seat and Grace's shoulder for a better look.

"Yeah, me too!" Lucy braced her arms on the dashboard and

rested her chin there while she took in the sight.

Grace got out and walked down the gentle slope to a relatively flat spot and sank down with an appreciative sigh. Dani and Lucy followed suit, and they sat for a few moments soaking in the peace.

Lucy drew in a deep breath and sighed. "Almost makes me forget about the horse's butt."

Grace rested her cheek on her drawn-up knees and grinned at Lucy. "Almost, but not quite?"

Dani reached over and lightly scratched Grace's back. "What are you thinking, honey."

"Mmm? I'm thinking I'll give you the rest of the day to stop that." Grace closed her eyes, enjoying the comfort her friend offered. She smiled when Dani giggled.

"He hurt your feelings, didn't he?"

Grace rubbed her forehead on her knees. "He did and it caught me completely off guard. Maybe I should have expected it."

"Why?" Lucy asked, puzzled.

"I'm a total stranger here. No one knows me."

"Whose fault is that?" Lucy demanded.

Grace waved away her question. "The point is, I show up one day and the next day Tobias is dead and I've inherited a small fortune." Grace lifted her head and sat back, bracing on her hands. "I just wonder if everyone is thinking the same thing as the sheriff."

They were silent for a few minutes, then Lucy said, "For the record, I'd just like to state that we have vastly different opinions about what constitutes a *small* fortune." She turned an impishly innocent face to Dani. "It's happened already. She's been rich a whole eight hours and she's already forgotten how the little people live."

Grace rolled her eyes. "Shut up, Lucy, you doofus." She had to work at keeping a straight face. "You're so crazy."

"If I was rich like you, you'd be calling me eccentric."

"I'll be calling you *walking back to the house* in a minute."

"Back to the original question…" Dani always stayed on track.

"Which is?" Lucy asked.

"Does everyone in town feel like the sheriff does, because if they do it's going to make for quite a hostile environment around here."

"Why is it anyone's business?"

"It's not," Grace answered, "but this is a small town, and both Tobias and Henry were fixtures here for over sixty years. One day after I came to town that changed. Violently."

"I know but you had nothing to do with that."

"Hmm."

Grace turned to Dani who looked deep in thought. "What, hmm?"

"I was just thinking, what if Tobias's secret was someone else's secret, too? You're an unknown and that person couldn't be sure that you would keep the secret like Tobias has all these years. It wouldn't do any good to kill you before you found out, so they killed Tobias before he could tell." She frowned. "On the other hand, I may be a complete idiot and have no clue what I'm talking about."

Grace thought through Dani's comments. "It makes sense in a bizarre kind of way - like something straight out of a suspense novel." She blew out a breath and stood, brushing herself off. "Okay, enough of this for tonight. My brain can't process any more and I'm hungry."

They walked to the jeep and piled in.

"How does potato soup and grilled cheese sound for dinner?"

"And a movie?" Lucy asked.

"Sounds perfect."

"I know just the one for tonight."

"Nothing scary!" Dani and Grace said at the same time, and laughed when Lucy rolled her eyes.

* * *

Zach pulled into the observation station that looked out over the gulf, and parked. He leaned his head back against the seat and closed his eyes, thankful to be the only one here for the moment. He had driven for hours, letting the speed of the car and the rhythm of the music leach the tension from his body. Unfortunately, his mind was not so easily stilled. Guilt ate at him for his harsh words to Grace Tucker. She hadn't deserved that. Or maybe she did, he didn't know. Until he did know more, that kind of response was out of line. He owed her an apology, and if he planned to get any sleep, it had to be made tonight.

He opened his eyes to one of the prettiest sunsets he'd ever seen. He hadn't prayed in a long time, but sunsets always made him think about God and where his life was going. As he watched the sun go down, the words spilled from his heart.

God, I know I have no right to pray or ask you for anything. I wouldn't blame you if you didn't want to listen to me, but I hope you will. I need help. I feel like something bad - something else bad - is about to happen. I'm in the dark here, and don't know what to do for the first time in my career. I miss Henry so much. Even when Mom and Dad died it didn't make me feel like an orphan, but I do now. I'm a grown man with a lot of responsibility and I feel like a little kid. I'm scared. Please help me, God. Help me know what to do.

* * *

"Soup's almost ready," Lucy said as she stirred the soup to check it. "Loaded?"

"Loaded," Dani and Grace agreed.

Lucy dumped in cheese, chives, and bacon and stirred again to help the cheese melt faster. Dani set drinks on the island while Grace flipped the last of the grilled cheese sandwiches onto a plate and brought it to the table. She grabbed a tub of sour cream from the fridge and they sat down to eat. Lucy and Grace peppered Dani with questions about Matt, and she was happy to talk about the man who had become the love of her life.

"Have you talked to him since you got here?" Grace asked.

"Please! She's practically living on her cell."

Dani didn't deny it and Grace grinned at her friend. She was so happy for her, and jealous, in the best kind of way. If anyone deserved to be happy in a relationship it was Dani. "Well, planning a wedding takes a lot of time and attention, you know."

Dani snorted. "I'm not planning a wedding. He hasn't even asked me. Yet."

"But you think he's going to?"

Dani looked at her soup for a long moment, then abruptly put her spoon down and leaned toward Grace and Lucy. "We looked at rings last week. He wanted to know what I liked."

They squealed, Lucy and Grace jumped up to hug Dani and they were all talking at one time when the doorbell rang.

"I'll get it," Lucy said. She twirled her finger around in their direction. "Please continue."

A few moments later Lucy returned. She was no longer smiling.

Chapter Eleven

Zach nearly groaned when the door opened. He'd forgotten the women who had been with Grace at Tobias's funeral. Her friends from home. He didn't need to ask if they'd heard about his comments to Grace. This one looked at him with the same disgust she would have for roadkill.

He tried for his best smile, fairly certain he was not successful. "Hi. I'm Sheriff Wells. Zach. I'd like to speak to Grace Tucker, please."

The woman nodded slowly, lips pursed, eyes narrowed, one hand on her hip, the other on the doorknob blocking his entrance. "I know who you are, and I'm not sure she wants to speak to you. Again," she added pointedly.

He took a deep breath. He deserved that, and on one hand he was glad Grace had friends that cared enough about her to be mad for her. On the other hand…

"I know she might not want to talk to me, and I don't blame her if she doesn't, but I'd like to hear it from her, if you don't mind." He managed to meet her accusing stare with his own steady gaze. It wasn't easy. She was a tiny woman, but he had no desire to tangle with her. He wasn't altogether certain he would win.

She considered for a moment, then stepped back. "Come on in, then. We'll see what she says."

Zach smiled. "Thank you, I appreciate it. Uh, sorry, I didn't get your name." The last was said to her retreating back. Zach blew out a tense breath and followed. He was now alone in the house with three women who were angry at him.

64

God help me.

Laughter bubbled from the kitchen.

That's a good sign.

The laughter stopped abruptly as he stepped into the kitchen behind the tiny lady. He tried to regroup mentally. He was an armed officer of the law, and bigger than all of them, but that didn't seem to matter one bit to the butterflies in his stomach.

He offered a smile to all three women, but focused on Grace. "Ms. Tucker, I'm sorry to interrupt your dinner, and I won't take much of your time, but I believe I owe you an apology."

Grace's friends stared at him, open mouthed, then looked at Grace. Zach couldn't read her expression and prepared to be shown the door. Then she surprised him.

"Have you had dinner, Sheriff?"

"Uh, not yet. I've been out most of the afternoon."

Grace slid from her perch on the bar stool, grabbed a bowl and ladled it full of soup.

"I didn't come here for that. I just came to talk for a minute."

She waved him to a seat and put a bowl of soup in front of him. "I have Coke and sweet tea. Preference?"

What in the world?

"Uh, tea, thanks."

The tiny warrior woman picked up her bowl and glass and headed out. "Dani and I will go pick out a movie for later while you two talk." She spoke to Grace, but watched him closely. "Call us if you need us."

He stared after her friends, totally at a loss.

Grace laughed softly, "She's pretty ferocious for a little thing, isn't she?"

Zach heard pride and affection in her voice and nodded. "Scared me a little."

She laughed again as she set a tall glass of tea in front of him.

Her kindness made him feel even more like an absolute jerk. He studied the spoon in his hand for a moment. "Ms. Tucker—"

"Please call me Grace."

He nodded. "Grace. I don't—" The words trailed off as he tried to get his bearings.

"Sheriff, my mother always said that a difficult conversation was a little easier when it took place over a meal. You haven't eaten yet and it's been a really terrible day for you. Grilled cheese and potato soup is one of my favorite comfort meals. Why don't you give it a try and we'll talk?"

He nodded and began to eat. In spite of his inner turmoil a sense of well-being began to slide in and he relaxed just a little. "This is really good."

She smiled and his stomach flipped again, but for a different reason this time. He concentrated on his soup. He had to say what he came to say or he'd never fully relax. "Grace, I do owe you an apology."

She put her spoon down, picked up her tea, sat back and waited.

He took a deep breath and jumped in. "I managed to control myself all day long, even with family, until I talked to you. There's no excuse for what I said to you and I'm truly sorry. It meant a lot that you came today. Tobias would have approved." He stopped and grinned. "He would have kicked my butt and had a few things to say to me if he'd been there to hear me spout off like an idiot."

To his surprise, she actually laughed.

He sucked in a breath. Was it such a beautiful sound because he was relieved or for another reason?

Not going there now!

The laughter faded along with her smile. "I appreciate the apology, Sheriff."

"Zach."

She nodded. "Zach. I appreciate it."

"But?"

"I've been thinking about what you said and—"

He held up his hand to stop her. "Grace, what I said was wrong. The minute I said it I wanted to take it back."

She nodded again, but now the smile was gone, and her beautiful green eyes were clouded with sadness. "I'm just wondering how many other people think that way. You thought it the first time we met, well, when you came back to tell us about Tobias and Henry. You implied that I had Tobias killed for money." She shrugged. "I don't blame you, really. I'd probably think the same thing in your shoes."

He spooned up another bite of soup. "Naturally suspicious?"

"Suspicious, cynical, whatever. You can't deny the circumstances are unusual, to say the least."

"No," he said thoughtfully. "They are unusual, but that doesn't mean something evil is afoot."

She choked on her tea. "Did you just say *afoot*?"

"Yes, it's a law enforcement term." He looked at her, all seriousness and innocence. "We use it quite frequently, actually. Why do you ask?"

He watched her take another sip of tea and try to decide if he was serious.

"So, am I forgiven for being a horse's butt?"

A tiny, surprised smile turned into a big grin.

"What?"

"I may have called you that earlier."

He laughed out loud for the first time in days and it felt good. "I deserved that."

"Yes you did."

"Are you always so agreeable?"

She smiled. "Would you like some more soup?"

"I'm good, thanks. It was delicious." He studied her for a moment. "You have an interesting way about you, Grace. Feeding the man who insulted you – it was the last thing I expected when I came here tonight."

She busied herself with the dishes. "Tobias thought a lot of you and Henry. That means something. I can't blame you for what you were thinking." She frowned and looked back over her shoulder at him. "How did you know about the inheritance so quickly? I only found out at ten this morning."

"I hate to admit it, but there's a secretary in the county clerk's office who likes to be the first to know things so she can be the first to tell. It wouldn't have stayed a secret long anyway, but she should have kept her mouth shut." He took his bowl and glass to the sink. "If it makes you feel any better I don't think she's told anyone but me yet."

"I didn't know anything about it, Zach, I promise. It's not why I came here. Before I got here I didn't know anything about him or his financial situation."

"Why did you come here, Grace?"

She popped a little cup in the single serve coffee maker and brewed a cup for him and then one for herself. He waited, not sure if she would answer, and he needed to know, for so many reasons.

They both perched on bar stools again, facing each other over the island. "He asked me to."

He cocked an eyebrow at her, surprised, and a little skeptical. "Just like that?"

"Yes and no." She blew across the top of her coffee and sipped carefully. "Is it important?"

"At this point everything is important. The state police are working on the shootings, but I'm doing my own unofficial investigation. I'm having a hard time figuring out who would want them dead."

Speaking of the investigation reminded him that he'd requested a background check on her, and he tamped down a surge of guilt for not telling her. It would be interesting to see if what she told him matched with what they learned from the background check. He hoped she was telling the truth.

"I was an only child. My father, Tobias's only son, became estranged from him and the rest of the family before I was born. When my parents died I was left with no family to speak of."

"What about your mother's family?"

"They were around sometimes, but not really. I don't know them so much as I know of them. It was a strange way to grow up. I don't know the cause of the estrangement; it was the one secret my father kept from everyone, including my mother." She caught and held his gaze. "I think Tobias was going to tell me what happened, and I think that's what got him killed."

Zach sat back in his seat, stunned. If something had happened to Tobias or his family years ago Henry would have known about it. If Henry knew, then he was as much of a threat as Tobias to someone out there, and it had gotten them both killed. Maybe. It was a huge assumption to make so early on in the investigation. Unfortunately, he didn't have any other theories to go on and this one fit. There was still the possibility that Grace had come to town to extort money from Tobias somehow, and ended up killing him for the whole shebang instead. He was not ready to scratch her name off his suspect list yet, but the more he got to know her the less he believed that she was involved.

He walked to the sink and stared out the window. "If you're right, then I need to find out what happened and how Tobias figures in." He turned to face her and leaned back on the counter. "I don't suppose you have any ideas?"

She shook her head. "Nope. Sorry." She frowned.

"What?"

"I think Doris knows. Every time I brought it up she got nervous and changed the subject without ever answering any questions. Have you talked to her?"

"Not yet, but I will." He grimaced. "That has the potential to be a very awkward conversation."

"Do you think I could go with you to talk to her? I really need to know what she knows."

He shook his head. "I'm sorry, Grace, but not on an official investigation."

She put her tea down on the counter and stared him down. "I didn't think yours was official. Aren't the state police heading this one?"

He sighed. "Yes, but it's more than that. You're an outsider here, Grace, and unknown." Some of the sparkle in her eyes died and he tried to soften his words. "Yes, Tobias invited you here and that should count for something. It will when folks get to know you, but it's early yet, and as you said, you got here one day and he was dead the next. The timing is bad because it happened before people could get to know you. It really is better if I talk to her alone."

She slumped back in her seat. "I know you're right, but I don't like it."

"I understand, believe me," he said with a wry smile. "I'm used to heading investigations, not sitting on the sidelines. It's making me crazy being out of the loop."

"Will you at least let me know what she says?"

"I can't promise that, Grace. Not without knowing what she will tell me."

A flare of temper sparked in her eyes. "Because you're not sure about me either, are you?"

It was more of a statement than a question. A very tentative truce has begun tonight and it was already being tested.

"I'm keeping an open mind for the moment," he said quietly. "It's the best I can do for now." He stood, prepared to leave. "I hope you will do the same."

He detoured to the game room on his way out to speak to her friends and waited as they paused the video and gave him their attention.

"Ladies, I owed Grace an apology, and I'd like to apologize to both of you as well." He enjoyed the surprise on their faces until it turned to suspicion. "Grace is very lucky to have friends who care enough about her to be mad on her behalf. I know with friends like that if you offend one, you offend them all. That's what I did today, and I'm truly sorry. I hope I can make it up to all of you one day."

He left them in stunned silence, wishing he could be a fly on the wall when the door closed and he was gone.

Chapter Twelve

Three days later, Grace hugged Dani and Lucy and all three cried a little when they left. They'd been with her for almost a week and had to go back to work. They needed the weekend to prepare and rest. Grace understood but she felt hollowed out inside, as if the best part of her left with them. She stood on the front porch and watched the car all the way down the long drive to the road and down the highway until it disappeared.

She was officially on a leave of absence from work. Jackson, her boss, had faxed papers for her to sign and they would be delivered to him Monday by Dani. She wandered back in the house – her house now – feeling at loose ends, ending up in the kitchen where she took care of breakfast dishes. She reached to put the little plates in the cabinet, annoyed that it was such an awkward place for them. It was not at all the way she would arrange her own kitchen.

A thought came to her and she gasped softly. *This is my kitchen.* She dropped into a chair and just sat. It was her kitchen, and her game room, and her study. She could look anywhere she wanted to, rearrange anything just the way she liked it. The whole idea was like a big pill that wouldn't go down no matter how much water you gulped with it. *What do I do now?*

She closed her eyes and focused on clearing her mind. What would she tell one of her counseling clients in a situation like this? *Make it your own.* A tiny trickle of excitement shot through her veins. She scanned the kitchen taking in every nook and cranny. Imagination sparked and she soon had the entire kitchen rearranged in her head.

Well, what are you waiting for? No time like the present.

Two hours later she fixed herself a cup of tea and sat back to enjoy the fruits of her labor. Every inch of the kitchen was sparkling clean and things put in places that made sense to her. She thought of Doris and what she would say. There wasn't a kitchen anywhere in the world big enough for two women.

She had a list of things to buy, and enjoyed feeling normal for the first time in many long days. Now she doodled on that list as she considered the next room she should work on. The thought of tackling the entire house dimmed the pleasure of her newly arranged kitchen. She placed her mug in the sink and headed for the study. Tobias had papers and files that needed to be sorted. She was a good organizer. It seemed like a good place to go next, and anticipating the view from the picture window made her feel a little bit better.

It had been easier sorting through things after her parents died. They had confided in her and trusted her to take care of things for them. Tobias was her grandfather, but for all intents and purposes he was a stranger. Try as she might, she couldn't shake the feeling that she was invading his privacy as she began sorting through his desk.

The phone rang and she answered without thinking. "Hello?"

"Ms. Tucker? Remington Forsythe here."

Amazing how a voice could instantly demolish a good feeling and replace it with dread. Grace grimaced, thankful he hadn't just shown up at the door.

"What can I do for you, Mr. Forsythe?"

"I'd like to schedule a time to come by and pick up Tobias's papers and things."

Chill bumps made their way across her entire body like a stadium full of football fans doing the wave. She didn't want to let him have anything from Tobias' office. It took a moment for her to remember that she didn't have to.

"Why?"

"I'm sorry, why what?"

"What exactly do you need, Mr. Forsythe, and why?"

"I'm your grandfather's attorney, Ms. Tucker," he said tightly.

Grace took a deep breath and blew it out slowly. She would not be bullied. "Yes, I remember. I'm just curious as to what specifically you might need?"

"Papers, Ms. Tucker. I'm afraid that's all I'm at liberty to say."

Indeed!

"I see. Well, I'm familiarizing myself with his business. I'm afraid I can't let you have anything until I'm finished going through everything." She heard him breathe over the phone. Hard. "If there's something specific you'd like me to watch for, I'll be glad to let you know if I find it."

"I'm afraid that's not acceptable, Ms. Tucker. Not at all acceptable."

Grace rolled her eyes. "I'm afraid it will have to be, Mr. Forsythe."

A long silence ensued.

"Ms. Tucker, I apologize for sounding so abrupt."

Indeed!

Every time she thought it, she pictured him cocking his head to the side like a little bird and spitting it out.

Yes, indeed!

"Thank you, Mr. Forsythe." Had she ever had such a civil conversation with someone so angry with her? "Is there anything else?"

"Uh, I think I should clarify my intentions, Ms. Tucker. Your grandfather was involved in some very delicate business dealings. There are negotiations that have reached a very sensitive state and must be attended to. There are papers there that will help things go according to his wishes and I really do need them. I'm sure you understand."

"I can appreciate that, but I don't think it would be very prudent of me to simply turn over all of his papers without knowing what is here first. I have no intention of doing anything that would cause problems for his businesses, and I assure you I can keep a secret. Anything confidential will remain that way. I'm sure Tobias had other personal papers here as well. I want to be sure those are dealt with properly."

"I'm afraid I must insist."

That's just enough!

"Mr. Forsythe, according to you I have inherited this property, the house, and its contents. I have a lot to learn, and I don't plan to make business decisions, including turning over paperwork to anyone, until I've had a chance to read over things and make an informed decision. I'm sorry that doesn't work for you, but as far as I'm concerned this discussion is over. Now if you'll excu—"

"I'll get a court order and force you to turn those papers over," he shouted into the phone, all pretext of solicitude gone.

"I'm afraid that's what you'll have to do. Goodbye, Mr. Forsythe."

Grace sank back into the big leather chair and stared at the phone. That man frightened her. She frowned. What did he want? One thing he didn't want was anyone looking through Tobias' files. Well that was too bad. She intended to read every piece of paper she could get her hands on and none of it would get turned over to that weasel. That thought led her to make two phone calls. The first was to Union Springs and her friend Mark Solaris. He was the husband of one of her good friends and an attorney, and she needed solid legal counsel. He promised to drive over in the morning. The second call was to a locksmith. Satisfied that those two issues were covered, she returned to the task of reading and sorting. This study held pieces of her grandfather's life and now it was the only way she had of getting to know him.

Grace was elbow deep in a filing cabinet when her stomach growled. She stretched and glanced at the grandfather clock that stood in the far corner of the room. She'd been working for over four hours.

She made her way to the kitchen and fixed a PB&J sandwich and a glass of tea and took it back to the desk. She nibbled while she opened the center desk drawer and poked and prodded through the usual office supplies. A little leather cup on one side held two key rings. Grace lifted them out and checked out the keys. They were too tiny to be house or car keys. A few looked like keys to a jewelry box or other small lock box. One or two could have been trunk keys or keys to an old-fashioned wardrobe. She dropped them back in the cup and closed the drawer.

Sorting had lost its appeal for now. She grabbed her tea and decided to explore the rest of the house for a few minutes. The study, kitchen, game room, and formal living and dining rooms were on the first floor along with two bathrooms. A butler's pantry connected the kitchen and dining room and Grace stopped to admire the china and beautiful serving pieces housed there. Moving to the stairs she climbed to the second floor which housed the master bedroom and five guest rooms. She shook her head. So much space. Each guest room had a sitting area, walk-in closet, and a large en-suite bathroom, complete with a spa tub. The only room she hadn't been in yet was Tobias's.

Doris had been the one to pick out a suit for burial. Even now it didn't seem right for her to go in. She paused in the doorway, taking in the scene. The furniture was dark and big. Heavy drapes covered the windows, one of which faced the front of the house with a view of anyone approaching. The adjacent wall had a window with a view of the east side of the property. The bed was against this wall. She ran her fingers over the stack of books on the nightstand as she caught sight of a black strap hooked around the bedpost. She leaned over, curious, and pulled on the strap until a pair of binoculars became visible.

Odd. She lifted the binoculars to peer through them out the window.

What were you looking for, Tobias? Or were you watching someone?

Unsettled but not sure why, she draped the strap back over the bedpost and moved to the closet. It was a huge walk-in, packed from one side to another with his clothes. At first glance it appeared that he had clothes from several decades. She sighed. Packing these would be a big chore but the local charities would be glad to get them. Well, most of them, anyway.

She closed the door and left the room for another day. At the end of the hall was another door, narrower than the rest. Behind the door, a staircase led up to the attic. Curious and a little nervous, she flipped the switch just inside the door, relieved when strong light flooded the space. She climbed to a roughly finished attic and had to smile as she stopped in the doorway. It was a treasure trove of family history. Trunks and wardrobes, a rocking chair, a baby buggy, furniture pieces that needed to be repaired and some beyond help. There were at least five boxes of books, some dried flowers covered in spider webs, hat boxes. Amazing. All the things you would expect to see in an old attic. It was picture perfect.

Grace walked over to one of the trunks and saw the latch had been padlocked. She knocked on the lid. It sounded full. She tried to move it. She could, just barely, It had to weigh a ton. The wardrobes were locked, too. She considered trying to find bolt cutters, then remembered the keys in the desk downstairs. They just might work.

She finished a quick look around then reluctantly headed back to the study. She had work to do right now, but tonight after dinner she would come back with the keys and see what Tobias kept in those trunks. They looked big enough to hide a body.

Chapter Thirteen

Zach looked up from his phone call to see Ross standing in the doorway. He waved him to a chair and gratefully accepted a cup of coffee as he finished the call. He sank back in his chair and took a long swig of the hot brew.

Ross stretched out his long legs and crossed them at the ankles. "It's way past quitting time. You planning to spend the night?"

Zach glanced at his watch. Eight-thirty. "One more stop to make before I head home."

"What's up and do you need help?"

Zach propped one booted foot on the desk. "No help this time, but thanks." Ross cocked an eyebrow in question and Zach sighed. "I'm going to talk to Grace Tucker."

"Oh?"

"I have some questions that need answers, that's all."

"At this time of night? What's going on Zach?"

Zach dropped his foot back to the ground and leaned over to pick up a file. He slid it across his desk and motioned for Ross to take a look.

"What is it?"

"Research. Background material on Grace Tucker. I asked Renee to check her out."

"Okay," Ross said slowly. "Any particular reason besides the obvious?"

"I need to know who I'm dealing with." He shrugged and sipped his coffee. "She's an unknown."

"And...?"

"She has a .380 registered in her name. Tobias and Henry were shot with a .380."

Both brows went up this time. "You think she shot them?"

"I'd like to see that gun and have ballistics check it out." He met Ross' incredulous look with his own steady gaze. "I'm keeping an open mind."

"So you're going to her house at eight-thirty at night to ask her about her gun? It can't wait until tomorrow?"

"It can. I can't."

Ross sipped his coffee and leaned back in his chair to scan the file. "Renee did good work."

"Always does."

Ross closed the file and left it in his lap. "I know it's hard for you not to be involved in this investigation - officially."

Zach scrubbed his hands over his face and pushed them through his hair. "I'm trying to stay out of the state guys' way, but I can't sit on my hands and wait for them to find something."

Ross' expression held sympathy and concern. "I get that. I'd feel the same way. I know we're talking about your grandfather and that's a special connection, but we're also talking about a man who was the sheriff here for decades. That makes him family to every cop who works here. We all feel the same, maybe for different reasons, but it's hard on everyone not to be working this case."

Zach stood and walked to the window that looked out into the bullpen. The shift had changed and most of his officers were out on patrol. One or two sat at desks writing reports. It was quiet for now.

"I've heard stories, you know, from my mom, about all those times that he was in a shootout or a high-speed chase. He was the negotiator in more than one hostage situation. He never got hurt on the job. Not once. Then he retires and gets shot in his own home. I can't wrap my head around that."

"What do you think? Job related or not?"

"If I knew that I'd be halfway to solving this case."

Ross tossed the file onto the desk. "Give me the short version."

Zach paced around the desk and dropped into his chair. "Thirty-two, never married. Has lived in Union Hill most of her life. She's some kind of counselor at a treatment agency for counselors." He held up his hands and shrugged. "I don't know what that means. Her father was Tuck's only child and left home when he was eighteen to join the army, cutting all ties with his family."

"Any contact at all since he left?"

"Nothing that Renee could find, so I'm assuming there was none. She doesn't miss things like that."

Ross nodded thoughtfully. "What else?"

"She's a good shot."

"How do you know that?"

"She's won some contests. Got a carry permit eight years ago and practices regularly." He met Ross' gaze and held it. "She's capable of making a shot like the one that killed Henry."

Ross leaned forward and rested his arms on his knees. "Impressive, but we both know half the county could make a shot like that, and some of them probably feel they have cause to kill either Henry or Tobias. I wouldn't bet a case on that."

"I don't intend to," Zach answered as he stood and grabbed his jacket. "But I do intend to check it out. Right now."

"How about some company?"

"Not necessary."

"I know, but I'm curious and I've got nothing better to do." He threw his empty cup in the trash and followed Zach out the door. "When you're done interrogating Ms. Tucker you can buy me dinner."

* * *

Grace checked the doors downstairs and flipped off the lights, ready to quit work for the night. It was after eight-thirty and while her body was tired, she wasn't ready to go to bed yet. She picked up her mug of hot chocolate and the keys from the desk and headed for the attic and a little treasure hunting. She needed a change from legal papers that were like trying to read Greek. She was so grateful for Mark giving up his Saturday to drive over and help make sense of everything. How strange that she could now afford to have a lawyer on retainer. She had no clue how to go about managing her inheritance and Mark's sound advice would be more than welcome.

In the attic, Grace chose a small trunk and sat cross-legged on the floor in front of it to try the keys. After brushing off years of dust and some rust, she started trying keys. Seven keys in she found the right one. Her excitement at finding her family history was tempered by the enormity of it. She was about to peek into a world that had held her curiosity for thirty-two years. Her hands trembled slightly and she dropped them into her lap and forced slow, deep breaths. Her heart pounded and her palms were sweaty.

Without giving herself time to change her mind, she shoved open the lid. Pleasure shot through her, calming her like nothing else could. It was her grandmother's wedding trunk.

"Oh my goodness!"

She carefully lifted a small, square pillow made of white satin, and lovingly fingered the light pink ribbons that had once secured wedding bands. The pillow and ruffles had yellowed with age but they were beautiful to her.

She gently set the pillow on the floor beside her and reached in again. A wedding album, yellowed like the pillow. The pages crinkled in protest as she turned them, the scent of old paper and dust tickled her nose. Tears filled her eyes, blurring her vision as she reverently touched a picture of Tobias and his bride on their wedding day. Her grandmother, Elizabeth. So beautiful. And Tobias, well, he was her father made over. Grace had to close the book as emotions overwhelmed her. When she continued a few minutes later she flipped through page after page of her family's story, studying each picture to find a glimpse of herself there. A sound pulled her from her thoughts. At least she thought she heard something. She looked around the attic. Probably the house settling. She put the album aside and was reaching for a small silver-plated box when something banged into a wall downstairs. She nearly jumped out of her skin. Every sense on alert, she froze, straining to listen. She heard a slight squeak and recognized the sound she'd heard all day long. Someone was in Tobias's study opening file cabinet drawers.

Her hand went to her pocket for her phone even as she remembered leaving it in her room to charge. The smart thing to do would be to wait here until whoever was downstairs left. If they were after Tobias's papers they would have no reason to look anywhere but the study. That reassured her until she thought of someone shooting Tobias and Henry. What if they thought she knew something? What if they wanted her dead, too?

She couldn't stay here. Whatever they were trying to steal must be important, and she needed to know what it was. She eased to her feet and moved carefully to the stairs. Sweat trickled down her back as she stepped carefully, wishing she had noticed if the stairs creaked. At the bottom, she paused to listen. There was no one on this floor, but she clearly heard someone moving around downstairs.

She made her way as quietly as possible to her room where she retrieved her handgun from her purse. The gun was always loaded and she flipped the safety off and grabbed her phone. She would call nine-one-one after she caught whoever was down there.

Light spilled into the hallway from the study. Whoever it was they were pretty bold to break in and turn the lights on. She peeked around the doorway and immediately recognized the intruder, even from behind. Fury ripped through her and for a split second she considered pulling the trigger. She stepped quietly into the room, raised her gun and aimed.

"Finding everything you need, Mr. Forsythe?"

Forsythe yelped and spun around, surprised but not terribly worried about being caught - until he saw the look on her face and the gun in her hand. She took great pleasure in watching the color drain out of his face. He looked like he was going to faint.

He brought his hands up and stepped back. "There's no need for that gun."

"I think an intruder in my home is always a reason for a gun," she replied. "What are you doing here?"

"I came for my papers."

"I see. The ones I said you couldn't have? Those papers?"

Anger made him forget the gun. "They're mine! You have no right to keep them from me!" He looked at her gun again and made a visible effort to control his temper.

"They were Tobias's papers. Now they're mine." She considered him for a moment. "They must be very important for you to go to this much trouble to get them."

"Very important."

"Maybe even incriminating?"

The little bit of color that had found its way back into his face fled once more. She'd hit a nerve. She pulled her phone out and started to dial.

"Who are you calling?"

"The police. I need to report a theft in progress."

Headlights from an approaching car washed through the room. A moment later she heard the sheriff call out.

"Grace? It's Zach."

Forsythe looked relieved until he saw her shaking her head slowly. He started to lower his hands but she motioned with her gun and he popped them back up.

"Back here, Zach. In the study."

She heard two sets of footsteps moving down the hallway.

"You all right?"

"Fine."

The sheriff stepped into the study. "Your front door's wide op—" He stopped when he saw the gun in her hand. His face hardened. Then he saw Forsythe. He looked back at her, an eyebrow raised in silent question.

A deputy she had never met stepped up to her and held out his hand for her gun. "May I?" He was polite enough, but it really wasn't a question.

Grace flipped the safety on, then handed the gun to him, butt first. She frowned when he looked at the gun, then at Zach. His nod was almost imperceptible but she caught it, and Zach's answering one.

Both deputies holstered their weapons. "You want to tell me what's going on here?" Zach stood in the middle of the room, his gaze locked on Grace.

"Mr. Forsythe decided to break in and take papers that I wouldn't give him earlier today."

"That's not true! I didn't have to break in, I have a key. Tobias gave me one a long time ago." He reached into his coat pocket and pulled out a key, holding it up for them to see. "Here, you want it back?"

Grace shook her head. "Don't bother. I'm having the locks changed in the morning. Obviously that wasn't soon enough." She walked over to the desk and started to gather papers scattered in Forsythe's search.

"Those are mine! Sheriff, I demand to be allowed to take those papers with me."

Zach looked around the room at the mess. "Can you tell me what even one of these is for?"

Forsythe sputtered and waved his hands around as if that explained everything.

"Please," she said. "Give me a break. You have no idea what you're stealing, you just want to get them before someone else has a chance to read them."

Rage lent an interesting hue to his pasty white skin. "I'm not stealing. The papers are mine, my business, attorney work product. It's highly confidential." He appealed to Zach. "I have a key, Zachariah. I didn't break in."

Zach sighed. "You may have a key, Forsythe, but it's not Tuck's house anymore. It belongs to Grace. That includes everything in it."

"Not my personal papers!"

Zach nodded toward the desk. "All those are your personal papers?"

"Well, I haven't had the chance to look at everything yet. I was going to take them with me to review."

"And what about the ones that aren't yours?" Grace asked. "Were you planning to return those?"

She didn't wait for him to answer but turned to Zach. "I'm tired, Sheriff. It's been a long day and it's not ending well. Are you going to arrest him?"

"Do you want to press charges?"

She looked around the room and back at both deputies. "Would it do any good?"

Zach started to answer but she waved him off. "Never mind. If he breaks in again I'll just shoot him myself."

The deputy had a sudden coughing fit, his lips twitching. Forsythe had the nerve to look surprised and offended.

"Go home, Forsythe," Zach said, "and leave your key."

"What about my papers?" he whined.

"The papers stay." Zach's tone left no room for argument. "If you don't like it you'll have to file a petition with the judge next week, but it's not happening tonight. And if you come back here I'll arrest you myself."

Forsythe stormed across the room toward the door, fury in his eyes. He was going to be trouble.

Grace went back to stacking and straightening files on the desk. She'd have to put them in order tomorrow. Tonight she was just too tired. She frowned when she remembered she hadn't made the nine-one-one call.

"Why did you come here tonight?"

Zach didn't respond immediately. He held out his hand for her gun and the deputy handed it to him then took a seat on the couch. Zach held up the little .380.

"This your gun?"

"It is."

"You have a carry permit?"

"I do."

"Has this gun been fired recently?"

"Three weeks ago, at the Union Hill firing range. It was my afternoon to practice."

"You any good?"

"I'm very good. Why are you asking?"

Zach looked her square in the eye. "I'm taking this gun in for testing. I'll give you a receipt."

Realization dawned slowly and in her heart she knew, and that knowledge made her sick. She made him say it. "Why?"

"A gun like this killed Henry and Tuck. Don't leave town, Grace." He turned and left. Left her unarmed, unsteady, and totally unprepared for what was coming.

Chapter Fourteen

Zach read the email twice. Lonnie, the ballistics tech, had done a huge favor for him and come in before seven to test Grace's gun. He was reading the results when Ross strolled in.

"I'm trying to decide if I've seen that particular look on your face before." He sipped a steaming cup of coffee as he studied Zach.

Zach glanced up and reached for the coffee Ross offered, then leaned back in his chair. "What look is that?"

Ross shrugged as he took the seat across from Zach. "Not sure. Frustrated? Confused?" He gestured toward the computer. "What's so interesting?"

Zach blew out a long breath. "Ballistics report."

Ross whistled softly. "That had to be the fastest one on record, at least around here. How'd you manage that?"

"Lonnie liked Henry." A simple statement that spoke volumes.

Ross nodded. "Seems like everyone around here is willing to bend over backwards to find out who did this." He looked pointedly at Zach. "You've got some good friends here, son."

"I know."

"So what does it say?"

"It's not the murder weapon."

"That's good, right?"

Zach didn't respond. He could trust Ross with anything, but Ross saw things too clearly sometimes, leaving Zach feeling exposed and vulnerable. Like now.

Ross propped his feet on the corner of the desk, prepared to wait.

"Yeah, it's good."

"That's what I thought."

Zach skewered Ross with a look. "What does that mean?"

Ross smiled and sipped his coffee. "It means you like her and you're relieved you won't have to arrest her for murder."

Not going there.

"It also means that somewhere out there one of my friends is hoping to get away with murder."

Ross' smile faded and he dropped his feet to the floor to lean closer to the desk. "You know how I felt about Tuck and Henry. It's personal for a lot of us. Everyone's thinking the same thing, Zach. Someone we work with or go to church with or play ball with killed them. No one wants to believe it, and it's gonna be a gut punch when we figure out who it is. In some ways it would be a lot easier if Grace had done it." His chair creaked as he leaned back. "So what's the plan?"

Zach shook his head. "Officially there is no plan. We stay out of the way and let the state guys handle it."

"Yeah, I know." Ross grinned at his friend. "So what's the plan?"

Zach smiled. It felt good to know he wasn't alone.

His secretary stuck her head in the door. "Breakfast order's ready in ten, boss."

"Thanks, Diane." He grabbed his jacket and grinned. "Ross will be in charge this morning. I've got some things to take care of."

Ross hurried after Zach. "Uh, care to fill me in?"

"I'm returning the gun," he called over his shoulder.

"And that requires breakfast?"

Zach pulled open his car door. "Peace offering. Wish me luck."

After a quick stop to pick up breakfast, he headed for Grace's house. When they'd left last night she was angry – and hurt. He grimaced at the twinge of guilt. He wasn't guilty of anything but doing his job, so why did he feel liked he'd kicked a puppy?

He would end up apologizing again and that sparked his temper. He made an effort to tamp that down. He was going to make peace. If that meant apologizing, well then, he'd apologize – at least for the situation.

He parked, grabbed the food and headed to the door. The doorbell sounded distant and off-key. Probably the batteries running down. He'd mention it. Maybe. He glanced at his watch. Eight-thirty. Maybe she was still asleep. He groaned softly. Dragging her out of bed was not going to help his cause. He waited another minute and decided she wasn't awake yet. Disappointed, he turned to leave and heard the door crack open.

He turned around and his hopeful smile faded. She wore the same clothes she'd had on last night. The slight bruising under bloodshot eyes spoke of a hard night. Her hair was messy and she looked like she was having trouble focusing. For a split second he wondered if she'd been drinking.

As if she could read his mind her eyes narrowed. He sighed. He hadn't said a word and she was already mad. Or maybe *still* mad. He had no clue what to say so he fell back on the food. He held up the bag and gave her a hopeful smile.

"I brought breakfast. Hungry?"

She stared at him without speaking, then turned and walked inside toward the kitchen. He hovered for a moment in the doorway, afraid of making a wrong move. She hadn't slammed the door in his face, which he took as an invitation, so he followed her inside. By the time he reached the kitchen she had coffee trickling from the machine and stood watching as it filled her mug.

He put the food out on the island and removed the lids from steaming plates. She took a deep breath and turned to see what he'd brought. He kept his smile to himself. He was on very thin ice here and didn't want to make a mistake.

At least she doesn't have her gun.

She held up a mug and raised an eyebrow.

He nodded. "That'd be great, thanks."

He opened the silverware drawer and found measuring spoons and cups.

She pointed to another drawer.

He pulled out two forks. "You've rearranged. I like it."

Her eyes narrowed for a split second before she turned to get his coffee.

They sat across from each other as they had before. He smiled at her and picked up his fork to dig in. It was halfway to his mouth when he saw her bow her head. He grimaced and lowered the fork to his plate while he waited. A moment later she picked up her fork, took a dainty bite, and sighed.

After a sip of coffee she spoke. "This is good, thank you."

He relaxed – a little. "Nothing like a trash plate from Waffle House. It has a little something for everyone." He smiled and took another big bite. Not sure what to say, he decided to let her lead. He could manage silence for a while if it meant he wasn't in trouble. He wolfed down his waffle and sat back with his coffee.

She played with her food for a bit, and he could almost see the wheels turning.

"Tell me about Tobias."

The question caught him off guard. There was so much to tell, years of stories to share, so many he didn't know where to begin, or what she wanted to know.

She took another bite, curious eyes fixed on him, waiting for a response.

She wanted to know her grandfather. He could do that.

"Tuck was a stubborn old coot," he began, and took it as a good sign when she smiled. He told her about Tobias's generosity and patronage of causes dear to him. He told her about the time he and Henry had gotten arrested together, and as many other stories as he could recall, happy to hear her occasional soft laughter.

When he stopped, she leaned back, cradling her coffee and smiling. "Thank you for telling me those things, and for breakfast." She slid off the bar stool and ran her hands through her hair, looking a little embarrassed. "I have some more questions but I'd really like to take a quick shower. Do you mind?"

He waved her out of the kitchen. "Take your time. I'm going to get some more coffee and take care of this stuff."

After she padded up the stairs, he braced his forearms on the island and exhaled heavily. She was giving him a chance. He had no idea why that mattered so much but it did.

He thought back to when she'd opened the door. How could she look so rough and so adorable at the same time? Best keep that thought to himself.

He threw away the food containers and dropped silverware into the dishwasher. Curious, he checked out the cabinets and drawers. Everything had been changed around, and though he'd hate to say it to Doris, it worked better. He shrugged. Must be a girl thing.

She came back downstairs more awake and put together, dressed for comfort in soft, faded jeans and an Alabama sweatshirt. Pink toenails peeked out from the bottom of her jeans and her wet hair was piled in some kind of curly thing on top of her head.

He tried to focus on the reason for his visit. She walked past him to refill her coffee and gestured for him to follow her when she left. The soft scents of her soap and shampoo pulled him like a magnet to the study. She smelled delicious.

She sat at the desk and he grabbed a wingback chair, swiveling it around to face her. "I'm sorry about last night, Grace."

She nodded, lost in thought.

He reached into his jacket pocket for her gun and placed it carefully on her desk. She looked at it, then at him.

"I assume since you're returning that I'm not a suspect

anymore?"

Not for me, at least. "That's right."

He met her wary gaze with his own steady one. "Despite our previous conversations, you've never really been a suspect, Grace. Can you understand why I had to be sure about the gun?"

"The state police questioned me, but they never asked about my gun. I don't even think they knew I had one. How did you know?"

He took a deep breath and tried to think quickly. The wrong answer could seriously damage the truce they had going. He finally decided truth was the best. "I had you checked out."

She cocked one brow in surprise. "I didn't think you were supposed to be investigating."

"I'm not. Officially." When she said nothing, he continued. "Henry was my grandfather, but he was more of a father to me than my own father was. I can't just sit and wait for someone else to figure out who killed him. I owe him more than that."

A soft smile lifted the corners of her mouth. "I can understand that," she said. "I can respect that."

He let out a breath he hadn't realized he'd been holding. "Thank you for that." He sank back in the cushioned chair and let himself enjoy the feeling of being understood and accepted. It was a powerful thing.

"Can I ask you something?"

He shifted in his chair. "Sure."

"What's the story on Remington Forsythe? Has he always been Tobias's lawyer?"

"Before I answer that let me ask what you think about him. I'm pretty sure I know, but—"

"I think he's a smarmy little lizard that belongs in a cage. He gives me the creeps."

Zach grinned. "Don't hold back. I really want to know what you think."

She laughed.

He lost his train of thought.

Not good!

"Smarmy. Yeah that fits." He laughed again, then sobered when he thought about the man standing in this room only a few hours ago. "I'm sorry he was here last night. Must have scared you, although, if I may say so, you didn't look scared at all when we got here. I almost felt sorry for him." She started to protest but he held up a hand to stop her. "Almost." He leaned in, full of speculation. "Would you really have shot him?"

She hesitated. "Off the record?"

He grinned and nodded. "Off the record."

She sat back and looked at him. "I was prepared to shoot when I came downstairs. I've been practicing and taking classes. I know how to protect myself. Part of me is relieved that I didn't have to shoot, but another part…"

"Thinks the world would be a better place without the Remington Forsythes of the world?"

She nodded. "I know it's wrong to feel that way. I believe life is sacred and everyone has a purpose…even chiggers have a purpose I suppose."

He couldn't help it. He belly-laughed at that and her disgusted expression. Soon, she was laughing with him until tears rolled down their faces.

She propped her face in her hands and took a deep breath. "Oh, that felt good."

He let his head fall back onto the chair and wiped his eyes. "Yeah, it did." He chuckled. "Chiggers?"

"In my defense, I could have chosen any number of annoying, disgusting creatures, any of which would be just as fitting." Her smile faded. "He really does make my skin crawl."

Zach nodded and stretched out his legs. "Mine, too. I've known him my whole life and I have to admit, I was surprised to find out he was Tuck's lawyer. Wouldn't have thought he would put up with someone like that."

"Why did he?"

Zach shrugged. "Who knows? I didn't understand a lot of Henry's friendships either. I supposed those old guys went through a lot together over the years. What is it they say makes strange bedfellows?"

"Politics."

"Right. Well, I'm sure politics figures in there somewhere along with the rest of the baggage."

"I think there's something here," she gestured around the room, "that he doesn't want me to find."

Zach frowned. "What do you mean?"

"The day he came to tell me about the will, he seemed to rush through everything like he didn't want me asking questions."

"Did he show you the will?"

"No. He gave me a letter from Tobias and told me about the property and the life insurance policy."

"You had no idea about that before then?"

Temper sparked in her eyes.

He held up a hand quickly. "I don't mean anything by that, Grace. I was just wondering if Tuck had a chance to talk with you. I know he wanted to. That's why he asked you to come."

She took a deep breath and let it out slowly. "He never told me anything," she said softly.

Her sadness reached him from across the room and an invisible hand squeezed his heart. "He wanted to, Grace. I'm sorry he never had a chance." He stood and walked to the window. "I'm sorry for a lot of things."

"I'm sorry I never had a chance to meet Henry," she said quietly.

He rubbed the back of his neck. "He would have liked you."

She smiled and it lit up her whole face and a little bit of his heart. "Do you think so?"

"Uh huh." He grinned. "He would have loved to see you holding a gun on Forsythe. It would have made his day."

"It made mine."

Zach rolled his eyes.

She laughed. "Guess I shouldn't say things like that to an officer of the law, huh?"

He chuckled, then sobered as a thought occurred to him. "You said last night you were having your locks changed today. Was that just for him, or is it true?"

Grace glanced at the clock. "They should be here in about an hour."

"Good. Get some deadbolts, too, while you're at it."

"I will, and I've got plenty of ammunition since I didn't have to shoot anyone last night."

"Good to know," he said wryly as the doorbell rang.

She grinned at him over her shoulder as she went to answer the door. He heard a man's voice and Grace's happy greeting. Jealousy punched at his gut as he heard laughter from the hall. He hadn't been jealous of a woman since high school. He forced a deep, slow breath and made a conscious effort to unclench his fists and jaw. He was not going to act like an idiot. He also wasn't going to stand here waiting to see who was making Grace laugh like that. He headed for the door as Grace entered on the arm of a tall, athletic, California blond who could have passed for a surfer. Zach disliked him immediately.

"Zach, this is Mark Solaris. He's an attorney in Highgrove. His wife is one of my best friends and she sent him here to help me sort through Tobias' affairs and deal with Remington Forsythe. Mark, this is Sheriff Zach Wells."

Zach hadn't really heard much after *wife*. He'd been too focused on forcing himself to act casual and unaffected. He extended his hand in greeting, sizing the man up, just as he knew Grace's guest was doing.

"Sheriff."

"Zach. Thanks for coming to help out Grace. I'm afraid she's been dropped in a bit of a mess."

Mark smiled at her and Zach's jaw muscle ticked. "Messes are my specialty. We'll get it sorted out."

Grace smiled up at him then waved him to the study. "I'm getting coffee. Zach, you need a refill?"

"No thanks, I need to get to the office." He picked up his jacket. "Mark, nice to meet you. Grace, call if you need anything, and keep this place locked up."

Chapter Fifteen

Grace waved goodbye and headed to the kitchen. Mark leaned against the door frame, a smirk firmly in place.

"What?" She moved past him and busied herself with the coffee.

He followed her and slid onto a bar stool. "You tell me."

"I have no idea what you're talking about," she said, but felt her face getting warm.

"It's a little early for visits from the sheriff, isn't it?"

She rolled her eyes and plopped down across from him. "It's not what you think. He was checking on me after last night, and he was nice enough to bring breakfast, that's all."

"Okay."

"And he had to return my gun."

"Excuse me?" All playfulness fled. "Why did he have your gun?"

Uh oh. "Um, he wanted to have it tested."

"Why?"

Oh, for heaven's sake," she said, exasperated. "It's the same kind of gun that killed Tobias and his grandfather and he wanted to ru—"

"Rule you out as a suspect?" He shoved his hands through his hair. "Grace, for the love of – did he have a warrant or read you your rights?"

Mark was a man of words, not violence, but right this minute he looked ready to do serious bodily harm to the sheriff.

"No, he just asked for the gun and I gave it to him. Mark, I did not kill those men, and neither did my gun. I had nothing to hide."

"That's not the point."

"What is the point, then?"

"It—" He exhaled deeply and lifted both hands in surrender. "Okay, look, let's step back and start at the beginning, all right? Why don't you tell me what's been going on since you got here?"

She needed him calm, not reactive. "I can do that, but let's sit in here where it's comfortable."

He took the coffee cup and followed her to the study, taking the chair where Zach had been sitting. Grace curled up on one end of the couch and cradled her mug as she started with the letter from Tobias and took Mark all the way through to his arrival. She'd known him for years and could usually read him fairly well. Today, however, he kept his expression neutral except for an occasional flash of emotion.

He leaned his head back on the chair, watching her through hooded eyes. "Are you sure you're all right?"

She smiled, warmed by his concern. "I'm fine, Mark, I promise. Last night was a little scary, but in the end I think Forsythe was more scared than I was." She smirked. "He never expected me to have a gun."

He shook his head. "Okay. Fine. What do you need for me to do?"

She hopped up and walked to the desk. A stack of papers and files sat there from the night before and she grabbed them and handed them to Mark. "I need to know what I've got here, and if it's important, what I need to do with it."

"Have you looked at anything yet?" He flipped through the pages in his hand.

"I started going through them yesterday. I've seen some tax things, old bills, stuff like that. I tried to sort and organize while I looked." She looked around ruefully and sighed. "It's a big mess. I'm sorry to dump it in your lap."

Mark grinned at her. "Don't worry, honey." He held out his

empty coffee cup. "Keep this full for me and I'll see what I can do."

"That's the best offer I've had all week." She headed for the kitchen, her heart lighter than it had been in a long time.

* * *

Zach strode across the grounds of the Cullen County Nursing Home in search of Sonny "Doc" Mullins. Old as the hills, Doc had been a resident of the home since before Zach was born. He knew the history of Cullen County better than anyone, mostly because he'd lived it.

Henry had often gone to Doc for advice or information during his tenure as sheriff. Doc knew everyone in town, their jobs, their family histories, their secrets. It was those secrets that Zach hoped to hear today. When he didn't find Doc at his usual place working on the raised vegetable gardens, he took his search inside and found him in his room, in bed.

Zach stepped up to the bed so Doc could see him. The eyes that looked back at him were glazed and unfocused. The slight tremors in his hands never stopped and for the first time, Doc seemed old to Zach.

Those glassy eyes homed in on Zach and Doc reached a shaky hand to pat Zach's arm.

"Have they found them yet?"

Zach frowned and leaned closer. "Found who?"

"You're Henry's boy."

"Yes sir, I'm Zach. May I visit with you for a few minutes?"

At Doc's brief nod, Zach pulled up a chair, swung it around and straddled it. He leaned in so Doc could hear him.

"Did they find them?"

"Find who, Doc?"

"Tobias knows. Henry, too."

"Okay. Can you tell me what they know?"

Doc turned his head toward Zach. "You're Henry's boy."

Zach dropped his head to the back of the chair. This was getting him nowhere. He raised his head again when Doc grabbed his hand.

"You send him to me. Tobias, too."

Zach shook his head slowly. Should he tell the old man they were both dead? "I can't do that, Doc. Tuck and Henry were killed last week."

That cloudy stare became laser focused. "He was going to talk. Had to shut him up."

A chill flashed through Zach's entire body and settled in his gut like a block of ice. "Who was going to talk?"

"Tobias. His secret to tell."

Zach took Doc's hand and squeezed hard. "Do you know the secret, Doc?"

The focus was gone again. "Not my secret to tell. Ask the girl."

"His granddaughter?"

Doc's sly smile made the hairs on the back of Zach's neck stand up. His chuckle was amused and smug. He suddenly laughed out loud, then abruptly stopped and stared straight at Zach. "Her secret now. She don't even know it yet, but she'll know it soon enough."

Chapter Sixteen

Grace took a seat in the back of Sally's Diner to wait for Mark. The lunch crowd had thinned out hours ago leaving her with the whole place to herself for the moment. By the time Mark arrived, Grace was helping herself to sweet tea and fried dill pickles. He slid into the booth across from her and tucked his briefcase under the table at his feet.

Grace handed him a menu and waited while he made his choice. They both settled on the meatloaf special, which came with mashed potatoes, green beans, a fruit cup, and a homemade buttered biscuit.

Mark caught her looking at a picture of a plate-sized brownie with a giant, melting scoop of ice cream, and laughed. "Wanna start with dessert?"

She nodded solemnly. "Yes. Yes, I do." She turned her attention back to him. His face held tension that wasn't there this morning, and light purple smudges under his eyes emphasized his weariness.

"I'm sending you back to your wife with some extra wear and tear on you. She's not going to appreciate that."

He chuckled. "It's been quite a full day, but I'm not complaining."

"Why do I get the feeling that you have the right to complain?"

"Because you're a very perceptive woman. Those counseling skills are not going to waste while you're on leave."

"Wanna tell me about it?"

He took a long drink of tea and sighed. "I spent a good part of the morning sparring with your favorite attorney."

"You were arguing with yourself?"

"Cute. Remington Forsythe."

She gave a mock shudder and made a face. "I was really hoping after today I'd never have to hear his name again."

His grin faded. "He's not going away, Grace. He's the attorney of record for your grandfather's businesses. As such, he has a legal right to all correspondence related to those businesses."

Grace huffed in frustration. "What about breaking into my house to rifle through things and steal stuff that didn't belong to him? He can't just do that, can he?"

"He should not remove anything from the house without your permission. The fact that he had a key to the house and apparently used it frequently when Tobias was alive, does not give him the right to use the key now that the house is yours, but it's a fine line, and I don't know that you want to pick that particular battle to fight just now. Besides, the locks are changed now, so it's a moot point."

The waitress brought their meals, refilled their tea glasses, then left them alone. They ate in silence for a few minutes as Grace processed everything he'd told her so far. But there was more. "So, what else do I need to know about your day."

Mark pulled a folder from his briefcase and handed it to her. She flipped through, scanning various legal documents, then closed the file, placed it on the table and waited for his explanation.

"Several things in there," he said. "First, a copy of the Power of Attorney. I've got one as well. I've got copies of everything, actually. I spoke to a financial planner friend this morning while I was waiting to see the court clerk. One of those pages is a listing of several recommendations for the money you inherited, investment possibilities, things like that. His card and contact information are in there. Look over everything, write down questions you have and then call him. He'll be available to you as needed, and you can trust him. He's been our adviser for years. Good guy."

Being responsible for that much money was overwhelming, and

Grace felt pressure to be a good steward of it. She pushed aside her plate and signaled their waitress.

Mark grinned. "Going for dessert?"

"Absolutely."

The waitress took her order for a brownie a la mode and coffee. Mark passed on the brownie, but ordered a large coffee to go.

"I still can't wrap my brain around the fact that I have two million dollars. What do people do with that kind of money?"

Dessert and coffee came and Grace dipped into the brownie immediately.

"Anything you want to, Grace. I know you love your work and there's no reason to quit. My best advice is that you not make any major decisions for a while. Pay off your mortgage and any other debt you have, then just sit on the money for a while and let the dust and your brain settle. People make the biggest mistakes when they go off half-cocked without thinking things through. And when long-lost relatives start coming out of the woodwork - and they will - tell them they have to talk to me if they're asking for money. I don't mind being the bad guy." He grinned. "I can do it so much better than you can."

Grace took another bite of brownie. He was leaving to go home when they finished here and she already felt the loss and the loneliness. As if he read her thoughts, his smile dimmed and he suddenly looked very serious.

She frowned. "What is it?"

"I don't feel entirely comfortable leaving today." He propped his elbows on the table and leaned in. "I feel like I'm leaving you in the middle of a bad situation."

She smiled to reassure him - or maybe herself. "It does feel like that. But I can't think of anything more you could do. You've sorted through things in the study and turned over the business stuff to Tobias's partner and Forsythe. I'll talk to the financial planner about the money and be thinking about what I want to do there. Maybe with all of that settled I can start letting everything else sink in a bit." She smiled at him. "I still feel like I've invaded someone else's home. Maybe I'll work on feeling more at home there. It's just going to take some time."

The attic. She'd not been back up there since the night of the break-in when she'd just begun to explore the history tucked away there. Excitement flashed through her as she anticipated continuing her search.

"What were you just thinking about?" Mark asked.

"Hmm? Oh, sorry. I was just thinking about getting back to the attic. There's some great stuff up there, pictures of my grandparents at their wedding, stuff like that." She shrugged. "Maybe it will help me get to know him a little bit."

Mark reached across the table to squeeze her hand in support. "I'm really sorry you didn't have more time with him."

She nodded, her smile sad. "So am I. It makes me feel a little like a fraud, taking his money and living in the house. It doesn't seem right. We didn't even know each other. Who leaves all that to a total stranger?"

"He may have been a stranger to you, but he kept tabs on you your whole life. I don't know why he waited until now to make contact with you, but he knew who you were, and he was proud of you."

She wanted desperately to believe that. "How could you know that?"

"Grace, I put some personal papers in a file for you in the middle desk drawer. I think they will explain a lot. Not everything, unfortunately, but you'll see he really did know you."

She took a deep breath to hold back tears that suddenly threatened. "Thank you so much for everything. You'll never know how much you've done for me this weekend."

He grinned. "Wait 'til you get my bill."

She laughed. "Whatever it is, it's more than worth it."

He slid out of the booth and grabbed his briefcase. "Come on.

Walk me to my car. It's time for me to hit the road."

He tossed his briefcase into the passenger's seat, grabbed her in a big bear hug, and popped a kiss on her forehead. "That's from Beth. She said I'd better take good care of you, so I'd appreciate a good report. I want her happy when I get home." He wagged his eyebrows and winked.

She laughed again. "No worries there. I'll make sure she knows what a good job you've done."

"Appreciate it." He turned serious. "We're not far. You call us if you need us, okay?"

She held up two fingers. "Scout's honor. Have a safe trip home." He pulled out of the parking lot and headed back home. She watched until he was out of sight, thinking about how many times she'd watched people leave. It was becoming a habit. She didn't care for it one bit.

Grace stopped at the grocery store on her way home. The pantry was well stocked so she just needed her favorite comfort foods. At home, she tucked them away for later and made a quick change into comfy jeans and an over-sized t-shirt. After checking to be sure the doors downstairs were locked, she headed to the attic.

Halfway up the stairs she stopped and ran back to her room for a notepad and pen. When no plans came to mind it was time to make a list. She was a champion list maker. Things to do. Things to buy. Things to research. She had lists for them all at one time or another.

Back in the attic she made a half-hearted swipe at a dusty old rocker before taking a seat and flipping open her notepad. Then she sat, her mind a total blank. Apparently total freedom came with some downsides. No structure and no direction. A tiny flutter of anxiety made her breath catch in her throat. She dropped the pad and pen on the floor and moved the rocker closer to one of the trunks. She came up here to explore, not to make herself crazy. There was enough here to keep her distracted for days, weeks.

The lock on the trunk opened easily and she lifted the lid, giddy with anticipation. It was loaded with tools of all kinds. She pulled them out one by one trying to figure out what they were. Some were familiar, but others were so odd she couldn't begin to make a guess at what they had been used for. Antiques for sure.

The next trunk contained fabric and ribbons, bolts of the stuff. Mason jars full of buttons lined one end. Boxes full of patterns - most over sixty years old - lay snuggled beneath the blanket of material. Her grandmother must have made most of her clothes. A roll of material was tucked into the side and Grace lifted it carefully, then closed the trunk lid and unrolled the fabric right there. Pieces of paper were pinned to the fabric. As she studied it, she realized it was a man's shirt, for some reason not finished. Had her grandmother been working on this when she got sick? If so, this little bundle of material has been here for more than twenty years, forgotten in the chaos of a catastrophic illness.

Grace picked up a piece of the shirt and sat back in the rocker, a bit overwhelmed with the significance of such a simple thing. She started to rock gently. Back and forth. Back and forth. The old chair creaked softly when she rocked back, the sound becoming a soothing distraction. She matched her breathing to the rocking. Inhale back with the creak. Exhale forward. In. Out. In. Out.

Jesus, what have you gotten me into? It's too much responsibility. What if I make a mistake? So many people have been hurt. I don't even know if Tobias knew you. Do you have him, Lord? I can't stand the thought that he might be lost forever. He needed me for something. I don't know what, and I have no idea what to do. Please show me what to do.

She jumped, startled from sleep when her cell phone rang. *What time is it?* She cleared her throat to answer the call.

"Hello?"

"Grace? It's Zach. You okay?"

"Uh, yeah." She rubbed her eyes and tried to focus. "I think I rocked myself to sleep."

"Okay."

She heard laughter in his voice. "What time is it?"

"Nine-thirty."

What? That's four hours. I've been asleep for four hours?

A glance out the window confirmed the hour. It was pitch black out there.

"You still there? You didn't go back to sleep on me, did you?"

A jaw-cracking yawn kept her from answering immediately. "No. Just surprised. I don't usually sleep during the day, and never for this long."

"It's been a busy week. You're probably more tired than you think."

"I guess so." She grabbed her pad and pen, flipped off the light and headed downstairs. She'd continue exploring another time. "What are you doing?"

"Just got back to the office. The rain caused a slew of wrecks this afternoon. None of them serious, thank goodness. Just a lot of paperwork."

"Rain?"

He laughed. "You really did sleep hard, didn't you? Yes, it rained most of the evening. Look out a window, Grace."

She made it to the kitchen and grabbed a Dr. Pepper from the fridge. "It's dark outside. I'll take your word for it." She dropped her pad on the counter and climbed onto a bar stool.

"What were you doing when you fell asleep?"

"Going through some things in the attic. I started that the other night but—"

"The night you almost shot Forsythe?"

She grinned. "Yep, that one. Anyway, I didn't get very far that night so I was going to try again. Apparently sitting down in the rocker was a mistake."

"I guess so. There's no telling what you'll find up there."

She smiled, remembering the few treasures she'd already unearthed. "I found my grandparents' wedding album. It was in a little trunk. It's great. He was so handsome and my grandmother was so young and pretty. I guess I'm looking for some history. My history." She sighed.

"What is it?"

"This must be how it feels to be adopted. You have a past, but it's just a blank. Now I have a chance to find some answers. It's a start, I guess."

He cleared his throat. "Well, that actually segues nicely into the reason I called. Maybe I can help fill in some of the blanks."

She sat up straight and her heart tripped a little in anticipation. "What do you have in mind?"

"I'm off Monday and thought you might like a tour of the property. There are a lot of pretty spots out there, some I haven't been to in years. I wouldn't mind seeing them again. The weather's supposed to be perfect, and it might help you to have a sense of the place." "I'd really like that, but are you sure you have the time?"

"Positive. I'm due a day off, and Ross can handle things while I'm gone. How about I bring breakfast, you fix the coffee? We'll eat and head out for the day."

It was a great offer and she wanted to do it more than anything. She looked at the blank page of her notepad, picked up her pen and wrote: EXPLORE.

"It sounds great. Thank you."

"That's a yes?"

"Absolutely. It's a date!" She gasped. "I mean, not a date, date. That's just a—"

His deep laughed rumbled through the phone.

"What?"

"You're cute when you're flustered." A pause. "As long as you're not armed." He laughed again. "Goodnight, Grace. I'll see you at six-thirty."

She started to protest the early hour, but he was already gone. A tour of the property. With Zach. A smile broke out and she found herself eager for a look at the land her grandfather had held so dear. If only that land could talk.

Chapter Seventeen

He was five minutes early but rang the doorbell anyway. He tried not to think about how much he looked forward to spending the day with Grace. From polite first meeting, to suspicious caution, to a kind of protective concern, he'd come full circle with her.

She was a puzzle that piqued his interest. Smart, funny, tough, and beautiful. He would have been interested anyway, but her ties to Tuck, and by extension, Henry, added another layer. They were tied together now, and he was determined to get to know her. Maybe together they could figure out what had happened and what the big secret was.

The door opened and he had to take a breath before he could speak. Her smile lit the hallway. She looked sleepy, but excited, and he smiled back. He didn't have a choice.

He held up a bag. "Your trash plate, ma'am."

She giggled and stepped back to let him in. "You say the sweetest things."

He stepped in and she closed the door behind him. In the kitchen, he opened the takeout containers while she got the coffee. Today he made sure to wait while she prayed.

"It's nice that you do that."

She looked up, surprised. "What? Pray before I eat?"

He nodded and took a huge bite. "Yeah. We used to do that all the time when I was growing up. I guess I got out of the habit once I left home."

"I did too, for a while. It's easy to skip it, especially when you eat alone." She took a bite and washed it down with coffee. "I had to relearn several habits after I'd been on my own for a while." She shrugged. "I guess I got lazy. I do it all the time now. It's a habit, like a morning time to read my Bible. I just feel better when I do it."

He gestured to the coffee pot. "You mind?"

"Make yourself at home."

He slid off the bar stool and popped a fresh pod in the coffee maker, then watched her while his mug filled. "You went to the community church Sunday. What did you think of it?"

She sat back with her coffee as she considered the question. "The music was great. I love the old hymns. It's what I grew up on. The pianist was fabulous! I've always wanted to be able to play like that." She grinned at him. "I can barely play chopsticks."

He laughed as he returned to his seat with his coffee. "Well you're in good company there."

She put her fork down and studied her food for a long moment. "Did Tobias go to church?"

It was important to her. He could tell by the way she asked the question and by her stillness.

"He did. More so in the last few years, but he was always doing something for the church." He pushed back his empty take-out container and sat back to finish his coffee. Deep concern radiated from her and enveloped him. It dulled the edge of happiness he wanted for today. It also touched him in a way that completely evaded every defense he had. He looked down at his coffee and frowned. He did not want to feel responsible for her. That was someone else's job. Then he remembered meeting her friend Mark and his frown deepened. He had been jealous of her friend. Her married friend. The friend who had come to be responsible for her.

He abruptly stood and walked his empty container to the garbage can and gave himself a hard kick in the pants while he went. How they had gone from easy playfulness to this was beyond him. He

111

needed to keep things light, for both their sakes.

"More coffee?" he asked before he took his seat.

"No thanks. This should keep me awake until lunch time. You're making a habit of feeding me in the morning."

He flashed a quick smile. "You know what they say, breakfast is the most important meal of the day. Especially when you have a big day ahead, and we do. You ready to get going?"

"Yes. Just give me five minutes and I'll be right down."

Where her sadness had reached him earlier, now her enthusiasm shone from her smile like beams of sunshine and warmed a place in his heart that he never realized had gone cold.

He leaned back against the counter, grateful for a few minutes alone. He needed to regroup. This was just a ride around the property. Not a date. Except it felt like a date. A very important one. Grace needed to get to know her property, and he needed to get to know Grace.

He made quick work of the cleanup and was done when she returned. She'd put on sturdy hiking boots and layered a sweater over her t-shirt. It was a little chilly this morning but as the sun came up it would be warm enough to shed a layer. Her hair was up in a ponytail, out of the way, and she looked perfect to go exploring. She looked perfect for anything.

He followed her out the door and waited for her to lock up. They climbed into his truck and headed off to do some exploring. He wondered just what they would discover.

* * *

Remington Forsythe had a huge desk and an even gaudier chair. He liked to think of it as the throne chair. He had them for one reason only. To intimidate anyone sitting across from him. The chairs across from him were smaller, and lower, giving his guests the impression of being somehow less. It didn't seem to faze the man sitting there this morning. It was only ten o'clock and he'd already been drinking. That concerned Forsythe. He had no moral qualms about alcohol consumption, but men had a way of spilling secrets when they drank, especially this man. They could ill-afford that kind of slip. Especially now.

"I thought we had an agreement that you would never come here." Forsythe glared at the man, annoyed to see it have no effect.

"We need to talk." He wasn't slurring his words. Yet.

"About what?" Forsythe snapped. "Everything is under control."

The man leaned forward and pinned Forsythe with a cold, hard stare. "You don't know that. You don't know what he told her."

"I told you, I have it covered."

"Really?" He sneered at Forsythe in disgust. "What do you plan to do, walk up to her and ask her what she knows?"

Forsythe was silent.

"You were supposed to get his papers. We don't know how much he's written down. What if everything is there in writing? It's as good as a signed confession. You were supposed to take care of that."

"It was out of my control!" Forsythe didn't bother keeping his voice down. He'd sent his secretary on a ridiculous errand and locked the doors so there would be no interruptions – and no one to overhear. He swore out loud and shot up to pace behind his desk. "She almost shot me!"

The man laughed. He slapped his hand on the arm of the chair as tears rolled down his cheeks. "I wish she had shot you." He continued until the laughter turned to a wet, bubbling wheeze. He pulled out a handkerchief and wiped his eyes between coughing fits.

Forsythe watched in disgust as he coughed hard and leaned over to spit into the trash can.

"You should be thankful she didn't kill me," he said quietly. "I'm the only thing standing between you and a death sentence."

The man instantly sobered. "Is that a threat, Forsythe?"

"It's the truth and you know it. We've come too far for you to blow it now. The drinking has to stop. Today."

"What do you suggest we do?"

"Nothing. Just like we've been doing. This is going to blow over and things will get back to normal soon."

"Really?" He rolled his eyes. "You think Tuck's granddaughter is going to go away and drop everything?"

Forsythe shrugged. "It doesn't matter. She can't learn anything if no one talks. Eventually she'll drop it. She'll have no choice. She'll go back to her job in Union Hill and everything will go back the way it was."

The man looked at Forsythe as if he were an idiot and snorted in derision. "She just inherited two million dollars and a lot of property here. You think she's going back to her job?"

"It won't matter." Forsythe repeated it like he was talking to a slow child. "Now get out of here and don't come back. And stop drinking before you become a liability."

The man walked to the door. "You may think you're protected in all this, Forsythe, but what do you think will happen to your practice if people find out you're up to your eyeballs in this? It's hard to practice law from prison, but I hear some people do. You think about that next time you decide to threaten me."

Forsythe watched him leave and sank back in his chair, more shaken than he wanted to admit. He'd seen it again and again over the years, the more people who knew a secret, the greater the chance of that secret becoming known. He'd kept careful, tight control for so long. It was unfathomable that now it could be unraveling right before his eyes. He cursed Tobias Tucker for needing to clear his conscience before he died. That had started this whole mess.

He opened the middle drawer of his desk and dug around for a bottle of Xanax, another relic of his secret-keeping days. He couldn't have a drink, he had court this morning and someone would smell it on his breath. Besides, one would never be enough. That would have to wait. He tipped two pills out of the bottle and downed them with a big gulp of water.

Secrets took on a life of their own, and a terrifying momentum when threatened with exposure. He had once witnessed an accident in which a train had crashed into a car stalled on the tracks. He'd seen it coming with the awful realization that he had no way to stop it. That same feeling pervaded his entire being now as he prayed for the Xanax to kick in.

Chapter Eighteen

Grace leaned back against a tree after she and Zach finished lunch. They had settled near the lake she'd found with Dani and Lucy, only on the other side. The sun was high overhead and she'd already shed her sweater as the day had warmed.

Zach lay stretched out in the grass, hands behind his head, eyes closed. He started to snore softly, and she smiled, completely relaxed. He was an excellent guide and it had become clear as the morning went on that he loved this land and had spent many happy hours here with his grandfather and hers.

She closed her eyes and let herself drift as she thought about their morning. Tobias had left her six thousand acres where he had once raised horses and cattle. Those animals had been sold and the land now leased to other farmers who had their own livestock on the property now. That gave her a regular income without the day-to-day responsibilities of caring for the land or animals. As they toured the property they met up with some of the people leasing her land and she quickly assured them that Tobias had encouraged her to continue their leases. She had every intention of doing so. They were good people. Hardworking. From what she could tell the land was well-tended. No need to mess with a good thing.

She couldn't wait to share pictures with Dani and Lucy. The land was beautiful and they'd bumped and bounced over a good bit of it, at times leaving the truck to push their way through overgrown brush. Her concern about snakes was forgotten as they pushed through a mass of bushes and vines to find an old outhouse-a one seater-complete with crescent-shaped cut out on the door. Vines wrapped the entire structure and rose into the air at the top. Zach offered to cut through the vines for her so she could open the door and see inside, and laughed at her not-at-all ladylike response.

Further down a narrow dirt trail they came upon a collection of hoses and coils and glass containers almost invisible under the vegetation slowly reclaiming that spot. She glanced up to find Zach grinning. A still, or what was left of one. She snapped more pictures and asked if it was Tobias's. No one knew. At least no one ever owned up to it. According to Zach, the woods on this property and Henry's were probably full of hidden stills from half a century ago.

She yawned, more relaxed than she'd been in weeks, and sleepy from the warmth of the afternoon sun. Her sweater made a decent pillow when rolled into a ball, and she curled up on her side, barely able to keep her eyes open. After a few minutes she quit trying.

When she woke, Zach was gone. As she sat up and stretched she caught sight of him standing at the edge of the lake. A glance at her watch told her she'd been asleep for a little over an hour. Zach turned back from the lake and joined her.

"When did you wake up?"

"When you started snoring," he replied with a grin.

She gasped, mortified. "I do not snore." She had no idea if she did or not, but for her own comfort she chose to believe not.

He smirked. "If you say so." He extended his hand and pulled her to her feet. It brought her face to face with him and they both froze.

She should step back. She didn't.

He should let go of her hand. He didn't.

Someone's heart was pounding. She chose to believe it was his. The stomach flip was hers. Definitely hers.

He raised his hand and touched her hair. He was going to kiss her. She shouldn't let him do that, but she couldn't think why. He tilted his head and stroked his fingers through her hair. She held her breath.

He stepped back and released her hand and held up a twig.

"You've got stuff in your hair." He said it casually, but his voice was soft and husky.

She reached up to run her hands over her hair and tried to regroup. "Thanks." She made a show of brushing herself off so she wouldn't have to make eye contact with him. They would just go on with their day and pretend that what almost happened hadn't almost happened. She needed to think about it, but it would have to be later, when she didn't have to look at him.

Zach gathered their lunch things and stowed them in the truck. Grace walked to her side and hopped in. Zach climbed in the driver's seat.

"Ready to see more?"

She nodded enthusiastically. "Absolutely. What's next?" She forced herself to act normal, ignoring the undercurrent still zinging through the air between them. She wished she could toss that away as easily as she tossed her sweater into the back seat.

"The bomb shelter."

All awkwardness fled as she turned her full attention on him, surprised. "The what?"

He grinned and put the truck in gear. "The bomb shelter. It was built in the fifties when the Cold War was still going on. Everyone was sure we'd be at war with Russia so they put in bomb shelters. Some were not much more than underground shacks and wouldn't have been much protection, if any, but I guess it was better than nothing."

"Is that what this one is, a little shack?"

"No. This one is a concrete bunker. Tuck had it built way back when. Henry built one, too."

"What did they use them for once the threat of war was over?"

He shrugged. "No idea. Probably just storage. Maybe not anything at all." He glanced over at her and then back to the road. "I've never been in them"

"Really?"

He nodded. "They've been locked up as long as I can remember. Probably before I was born."

"Did you ever ask about them?"

"Yeah, but Tuck would never take me. Henry wouldn't take me to his either. He just said there was a lot of old, useless stuff down there that I didn't need to be playing around with." He grinned at he again. "I always thought they'd make great forts."

She laughed and thought how much little boys would love having a place like that to play. "Like the Batcave."

He grinned and nodded. "Exactly."

They drove for several minutes in silence. "I've lost my bearings a bit. Are we far from the house?"

"We're about three miles west of the house. The bunker is a mile on the east side."

She frowned. "That seems pretty far away. I don't know anything about shelters but it seems like you'd want it closer, in case you had to make a run for it."

"Yeah, I don't know. That would make sense."

"How do you know where it is? Is there a marker or flag or something?"

"There's an old building that used to be a workshop. It had electricity running to it at one time. Maybe it still does. Once you get to that building you can see the very top of the bunker. It's almost like the things on a submarine, you know, the conning towers. It sticks up a little. That's where you enter the bunker. It's thick, reinforced concrete. The rest is underground."

"When was the last time you were here?"

He drew in a deep breath. "Wow. Probably when I was in high school. I pestered Tuck about taking me down there for years. I guess I finally gave up."

He turned onto a hard-packed dirt path in danger of being taken back by the surrounding woods. It didn't appear that anyone had been here in years. Grace's pulse sped up in anticipation, and moments later the old workshop became visible through the trees. It looked neglected, but surprisingly solid. The power pole stood several yards off the back side of the buildings, lines still intact.

Zach parked and Grace jumped down to follow him around the building. She turned the corner and got her first glimpse of the bunker. Her breath caught and she stepped up next to Zach to see more.

Another part of her past. Her family, fearing the outbreak of nuclear war, had built a shelter out in the middle of their property. Was it hidden so neighbors and townspeople couldn't find it and demand to enter? She frowned. Not a great thought to have about your family.

Zach walked ahead and climbed onto the concrete base around the tower. She joined him and he handed her up, both of them careful to keep some distance this time. She felt the beginnings of a blush and turned away so he wouldn't see.

A heavy-duty hasp was secured by a chain made of thick links wrapped several times through the loop. It was held in place by a huge padlock. Grace wondered how many pounds the whole contraption weighed. Curious, she reached over to lift the lock.

"Wow! I didn't know they made locks this big."

Zach flipped it up to check the bottom. It was dirty and rusty, not surprising considering the length of time it had been exposed to the elements. The lock itself had dirt and other bits of debris in it. "Hmm. I bet even if we could find a key for this we'd never get it to work." He paused and looked at Grace. "Do you want to get some equipment and open it up?"

She looked up, surprised. "Do you think we should?" Extreme curiosity had gotten her in trouble more than once. She just couldn't help herself. Oh, but she really wanted to see inside.

He smiled and shook his head. "I guess it's going to take some time, huh?"

"What?"

He raised his arms and looked at the land around them. "This is yours now, Grace. You can do whatever you want to."

She opened her mouth to respond, then couldn't think what to say. She did keep forgetting that. She had felt like a visitor all day. Would it ever feel like home? Her mind flashed back to the kitchen, now organized the way she liked it.

Make it yours, Grace. Make it all yours. Then it will feel like home.

Zach quietly watched her work it out. She smiled, her decision made. "I *can* do whatever I want, can't I?"

He grinned and nodded. "Your wish is my command."

She took a deep breath. "Let's open it!"

His face lit up like a kid at Christmas. "Okay. I need to bring some equipment with me to cut the lock. Not sure how long that will take, and we want to have time to explore once we get in. I hate to say this, but we need to start earlier in the day when we come back."

"When?"

He laughed. "Some of us have to work once in a while."

She heaved a dramatic sigh and pretended to pout. "Oh well, I guess I can wait." She rubbed her hands together gleefully. "But not for long."

Zach headed the truck toward the house and they spent the drive making a list of what they would need for their next visit to the bunker. The sun was going down when they reached the house. Grace's taste for exploring had kicked into overdrive and she couldn't wait to get back to the attic.

"I had a really great time today, Zach. Thank you for suggesting this."

"You're welcome. It was fun for me, too. I'd forgotten how pretty some of this land is. It was great to see it again with someone seeing it for the first time."

She held up the list of supplies they'd compiled. "Want me to see what Tobias has around here?"

"If you want. I have everything on the list but if you have some things here I won't have to haul so much."

He smiled as if he understood her impatience. She knew he did.

"I may be able to play hooky this Thursday if Ross can cover for me again. I'll let you know later in the week. Will that work for you?"

She worked to keep her excitement in check. "Thursday is fine."

"Great. It's a date." He grinned. "Well, not a date, date—"

She narrowed her eyes at him, embarrassed but trying hard not to laugh. "Shut up, Zach. Go away."

She slid out of the truck and listened to his laughter as he drove away.

Grace, you are in so much trouble!

Chapter Nineteen

Dani received a full report on Grace from Beth after Mark got home, but there was nothing like firsthand intelligence. She dialed Grace's number, anxious to see for herself how her friend was doing.

"Hello?"

"Hi, honey. How's it going?"

"Dani! I'm so glad you called." Grace's sigh drifted through the phone connection. "I miss you guys so much."

Dani snuggled down into her big overstuffed chair and pulled a throw over herself, chilled by the evening breeze coming through the open window. "We miss you, too, sweetie. Lucy said to say hello for her."

"What's she doing tonight?"

"She's got her Red Cross support group at the church. You'll probably get a call from her tomorrow night, but tonight I have you all to myself."

Grace giggled and Dani relaxed a bit. Beth had told her that Grace was starting to settle in and get her bearings. She sounded happy and relaxed tonight and Dani took that as a good sign.

"I'm all yours. What's happening with you? Has Jack piled my whole caseload on you?"

Dani laughed. "Actually, he's taken some of the load himself, and delegated the rest. He said he needed to practice so he didn't get rusty."

Grace snorted. "Like that would ever happen. He's the best clinician I know."

"I know. He doesn't need the practice. I think he secretly likes being in the middle of the chaos. Anyway, he's taking good care of your patients." She paused. "Are you missing work yet?"

"I don't know. I haven't really had time to think about it. That sounds bad, doesn't it?"

"Not really. Mark told us everything that's been happening. Makes my head spin. I'm not surprised you haven't had time for anything else."

"Makes my head spin, too."

"Oh, Grace," Dani said as a memory hit her. "I would give anything to have seen you hold a gun on that weasel, Forsythe! Please, tell me everything. Start at the beginning."

Dani listened to Grace talk for the next few minutes. It made her a little sad that things were changing so much. She didn't do change well, and she didn't have many close friends. Grace was one of the few, and although Dani knew change was inevitable, she never could feel totally comfortable with it.

"Okay," Grace said finally. "You're caught up on my life, now catch me up on yours, specifically Matt."

Dani sighed happily and stared at Matt's picture on the table next to her. "He's wonderful," she said softly as she smiled. "We've got a special date planned for Friday night. I think he's going to pop the question."

Grace squealed and almost popped Dani's eardrum before she could yank the phone away. That more than anything convinced her that Grace was okay.

"I'm so happy for you. He's such a great guy."

"I know. It still doesn't seem real. So much has happened in such a short time."

"Tell me about it."

Dani laughed. "Yeah, you're getting a good dose of that, aren't you?"

"Uh huh. Things are better since Mark was here. I promise you, Dani, I'd be so lost if he hadn't waded through everything for me. Beth is an angel for sharing him."

"She thought you might be able to use his help. So, tell me about the horse's butt."

Grace laughed out loud. "He's actually had a change of attitude. I spent the day with him today, exploring the property. You wouldn't believe what we found out there. I'll send you pictures."

"Wow. Okay. That's pretty amazing. What brought about that change?"

"I don't know. Maybe he's had time to think. Maybe having my gun tested and confirming that I didn't kill our grandfathers made him think twice. I don't know."

"He had your gun tested?" Dani's temper flared. "He actually thought you killed them?"

"Yes, but in his defense he was probably thinking more like a grieving grandson than a cop. And he doesn't know me. Or didn't."

Dani blew out a long breath. "You sound like you've forgiven him."

"I guess I have. He's made an effort to be nice and it's been…nice."

"Explain, please."

"He's been trying to help me fill in the gaps about Tobias. I'm getting to know him a little better through the stories Zach is telling me."

Dani heard the wistfulness in her voice. "I'm glad, honey. I know you need that. I just don't want you to get hurt."

"I don't want me to get hurt either." Grace sighed softly. "I think he's interested, and I like him. We had a great time today. He's funny and thoughtful. I'm not in a hurry, just enjoying the company right now."

"That's smart. Hey, Lucy and I are thinking about making a trip over this weekend. Does that work for you?"

"Oh, I'd love that. I hope you can."

"I'll check with her tomorrow and let you know." She paused for a moment. "You take care of yourself, Grace. Are you sure you're all right?"

"I'm trying to figure out where I'm going with everything that's happened. I've never felt so unprepared for anything in my life." She blew out a long breath. "It's hard for me to hear God right now, you know?"

Dani nodded. "I totally get that. I remember something a wise friend told me not too long ago."

Grace laughed. "And what was that?"

"When God is silent it's because he's giving me time to talk things out and think about what he's already told me. So, I need to keep talking until he's ready to answer."

"Hmm. She must be a very wise woman."

"She thinks she is." Dani smiled when Grace laughed. "She does all right most of the time."

Dani hung up, grateful that for now Grace seemed to be managing all right. Adjusting to a new normal was hard. Dani knew that as well as anyone. Grace was strong and had been her rock when Dani needed her. Now she prayed she could repay that gift as effectively as it had been given to her.

* * *

Grace woke Wednesday morning with a plan. After a quick trip to the grocery store she had several empty boxes and a roll of extra-large, heavy-duty garbage bags. She grabbed Pop-Tarts and a Dr. Pepper and headed to Tobias's bedroom. She munched on a Pop-Tart as she sorted through his clothes. She knew this was usually a very emotional task for loved ones but she felt no attachment to his clothes.

No grief about giving them away, and that, in itself, was sad.

She shook it off and made quick work of the closet. Her organized soul insisted on packing like with like. She carefully folded dress slacks and began to fill one bag, then loaded another with dress shirts. Jackets and coats tucked into a garment bag. She managed to collect all of his shoes in one large box. When all the clothes from the closet were packed, she slid the boxes and dragged the bags to the top of the stairs to take down later.

Coming back to the closet, she pulled boxes from the shelves and took them to the bed so she could sit and explore. She flipped the lid off the first box which held a collection of silver belt buckles. They were commemorative and so big she couldn't imagine anyone actually wearing them. She put the lid back on and moved to the next box. This one contained old photographs. She recognized some of the photos as duplicates of the ones she'd found in the attic. Each of the five boxes contained a different facet of her grandparents' lives. She wouldn't be getting rid of those, and didn't want to rush through them, either. She carefully replaced them in the closet, leaving them for another time.

She slid and dragged her boxes and bags down the stairs and against the wall in the hallway. Next, she headed back to the attic. The windows let in the early morning light and Grace slid them open as far as they would go. It was still a bit chilly but the attic needed to be aired out, and she was about to stir up a lot of dust.

She shook open a garbage bag and pulled open a box to begin her search and purge. The box itself was brittle and the tape that once secured it had hardened and yellowed until it was useless.

First out of the box, bundles of dried flowers, dusty, crumbly, and beginning to mold. She dropped them into the bag. Wrappers from candy and empty popcorn bags littered the box. Probably mementos from happy times, they meant nothing to Grace, and she discarded them as well.

One by one she made her way through boxes and trunks. She

stacked books along one wall to be looked at later. Old toys went into a box to be donated except for the ones that appeared to be handmade. Her grandmother's work, no doubt, and she would find a place to display them throughout the house. A box full of letters tempted her to stop working and read, but she was determined to keep up the momentum of cleaning and purging. She pushed the box to the side. Those could be read in the evenings after she finished cleaning out.

A flat box caught her eye and she dragged it out and sat on the floor to open it. She lifted the lid to find the most beautiful paintings she'd ever seen. She held her breath as she flipped through the beautiful, vibrant depictions of various places on the property. She recognized several places she'd seen with Zach earlier in the week. Each one was signed *Elizabeth Tucker.* Her grandmother. Why were they not framed and hanging in the house?

Grace closed the box and slid it over to the pile of things she would spend more time with later. She stretched and hauled several bags of garbage downstairs, took thirty minutes to make chocolate chip cookies from a roll of refrigerator dough and headed back upstairs with a plate of warm, freshly baked treats.

She found a trunk of records for an old Victrola, and yearbooks from Cullen County High School from the nineteen forties. She assumed the garment bag of women's clothes must have been her grandmother's, since she had found no ladies' clothes in Tobias' closet.

She moved quickly on this first pass through the attic. When she stopped for a break it was mid-afternoon and she had worked through lunch. Now that she was aware of the time she was not surprised to hear her stomach growl. A plate of cookies and Pop-Tarts were the sum total of her nutritional intake today. Time for some real food.

A second flat box caught her eye as she made her way to the stairs. She assumed it would contain more of her grandmother's paintings so she grabbed it and headed downstairs to look through while she ate.

She sautéed veggies and chicken and put the mixture over pasta, poured a glass of tea and sat at the kitchen island to eat and look at her grandmother's paintings. She took a bite and reached for the box, flipping open the lid carefully. Instead of pictures the box held yellowed newspaper clippings. She lifted the first one and scanned it.

A local man had disappeared on his way home from work. There had been no signs of the man or his vehicle. It was as if he'd vanished into thin air. Grace stared at the date.   Over forty years ago. Adrenaline raced through her system. She started at the beginning again and this time read every word. There was not one mention of Tobias and not one hint that this was in any way connected to her family. Her mind grabbed for the logic of that, but her stomach twisted into one big knot.

She pushed her plate away and lifted out the next aged piece of paper. For the next twenty minutes she read and reread every clipping in the box. The last one made her heart ache. Four men had disappeared. The article in her hand now cited a fifth victim. Martin Tucker. The article contained a quote from the victim's brother – Tobias Tucker:

On behalf of the family I'd like to thank everyone for their kind words and prayers as

we continue the search for my brother. Our community has been devastated by the

disappearance of these five men, and we are all trusting the agencies involved to find

them and return them to us safely.

Nausea roiled through her. She dropped her head to the counter. *You're not sick, just breathe.* It took a few minutes for her to risk lifting her head and sitting up straight. She considered herself a strong woman, but the swings from one emotional extreme to another were proving to be more than she could manage.

Exhaustion, emotional and physical, settled into her body and brain like wet cement. She needed to sleep but knew that wouldn't happen until she could talk about what she'd found. She reached for her cell and called the newest number in her contact list, the only other person who would understand.

* * *

Zach looked up from the paperwork on his desk when Ross stepped through the door and put a mug of coffee on his desk. Zack waved him to a seat and drank deeply of the hot, strong brew. No one made coffee like Ross, for which most people were grateful. Today, Zach appreciated and needed the extra caffeine kick.

"Monthly commissioner's report?"

"How'd you guess?" Nothing exhausted him like paperwork. He could work for forty-eight hours straight on a case, had done so many times. In a strange way it energized him. The exact opposite was true of paperwork, no matter what kind. It came with the job but he hated it. Give him a good bar fight to break up or a break-in to investigate any day of the week. Please.

He closed the report folder and sat back with his coffee, allowing himself five minutes to discuss the day with his deputy chief. "How was shift change?"

"Went like clockwork." Ross sipped his coffee and studied Zach. "I haven't had a chance to ask about your day with Ms. Tucker."

Zack took his time answering. Ross knew almost everything about him – mostly because he was nosy, but if Zach asked for privacy Ross would respect that. He could at least hit the high spots.

"It was good. We covered most of the property. She took lots of pictures and met some of the folks leasing her land. That seemed to go well. Her lawyer sent letters to everyone telling them officially that they can keep using the land, but she told them in person. I think she made a good impression."

"It appears that she did."

He was all innocence when Zach stared him down.

"We went to the bunker." Zach knew that would grab Ross' attention. He had wanted to go there as much as Zach when they were kids.

"Really? Did you open it?"

"No, but she wants to." He grinned when Ross' eyes lit up. "I think we're going to try to open it Thursday if someone will cover for me."

Ross raised his hand. "I can cover for you."

"That's very generous of you, friend."

"Yes it is, and to show that I'm a very involved officer of the law, I will even make the effort to drive by to be sure that the scene is safe and secure for exploration."

Zach put his hand over his heart. "Yet another selfless gesture."

Ross inclined his head in acknowledgment. "It's the least I can do."

Ross drank the last of his coffee and tossed the cup into the garbage can. "How are things coming with Henry's estate?"

"Okay, I guess. He'd already added my name to the properties he wanted me to have and I'm beneficiary on some of his insurance policies. Not much to do with those. There are still some things the attorney is working on."

"Not Forsythe, I hope."

Zach rolled his eyes. "Not Forsythe. I never did understand what Tuck was doing when he hired that guy. I don't think he trusted him. I know Henry didn't."

Ross shrugged. "Who knows? All those old guys had weird business arrangements back then. Maybe Forsythe was different then, you know. Decent?"

They stared at one another for a minute. "Nah," they said in unison.

Ross stood and stretched. "I'm going home. Keep your head down out there. Call me if you need me."

"I will. Thanks, man. Have a good night."

Zach waved goodbye as his cell phone rang. He flipped it over to look at the caller ID, prepared to screen the call and let it go to voice mail. Grace's name appeared in the window. He ignored the stomach flip and answered.

"Hi, Grace. How's the attic exploration going?"

There was a slight pause. "Zach?"

He sat up and leaned forward as if that could help him hear better. "What's the matter? Are you okay?"

"I found something in the attic today. I know it's late and you're probably ready to go home bu—"

"Do you need me to come over?"

"I'd really appreciate it. I think you should see this."

"Okay. I can be there in about fifteen minutes. Are you sure you're okay?" She sounded weird and he was tempted to ask what she'd found, but he decided it was best to just get there and see for himself. He knew it was important. She would never have called him otherwise."

"I'm fine. I'm sorry. I know this sounds crazy—"

"Grace, it's fine. I was about to leave the office anyway. I'll be there in a few minutes."

He grabbed his jacket and headed to the car. He tried not to feel too happy that she'd called him instead of someone else, not that there was anyone else she could call here. Besides, if what she found involved their grandfathers, who else would she call anyway?

Chapter Twenty

She answered the door as he rang the bell and motioned for him to follow her. She led him to the kitchen where a tattered box sat on the island counter, and a scattering of newspaper clippings covered the surface.

"Thanks for coming."

"What is all this?"

"You should just read them. Would you like some coffee?"

He nodded as he shrugged out of his jacket. "I have a feeling I'm going to need it. Thanks."

She put the coffee in front of him but it was forgotten after the first sip as he started reading. He sensed her watching him while he read which distracted him at first. The more he read, the less aware he became of the kitchen and Grace. His pulse bounded as adrenaline surged. This was what he had been looking for in the archives at the newspaper office.

He read everything twice. She did not interrupt, waiting patiently for him to finish. As he looked up at her, he realized it was not patience as much as exhaustion that kept her sitting there quietly. He sat back with his now lukewarm coffee.

She looked directly at him. "Did you know?"

Last week he would have been insulted by that question and fired back at her. Today he knew her better and understood why she had to ask. "No, Grace. I promise on my honor, this is the first I've heard of this."

She studied his face, then nodded.

"Did they ever find them?"

He inhaled sharply. Doc had asked him that only days before. *"Have they found them yet? Tobias knows. Henry, too."*

"What is it?"

He had to tell her about Doc. They were in this mess together, whatever it was. Somehow the sins of the grandfathers were coming to rest on the grandchildren.

"Someone else asked me that same question a few days ago." He told her about his visit with Doc Mullins and their strange conversation. "I had no idea what he was talking about at the time. He couldn't explain, he just kept saying that Tobias and Henry knew."

"Anyone with access to a newspaper would have known about the disappearances." Her gaze held his. "That wasn't what he meant when he said they knew. It was something else. Something worse."

He looked at the clippings again, stopping on the one about Martin Tucker. "I never knew Tuck had a brother. He never mentioned it, and I never saw anything to indicate he had other family."

He watched her process that for a few moments. He liked how her mind worked. She was sharp and witty, but now also tired and very sad. She started to speak but stopped, uncertain.

"What are you thinking?"

She shook her head and stared at the clippings, tapping her finger on the counter with nervous energy.

"C'mon. Out with it."

She picked up the clipping on Martin again and held it out as though to study it. "Can I ask you a question first?"

"Shoot."

"Do you have any pictures of Henry?"

He cocked a brow. *Where is she going with this?* He pulled his wallet from his back pocket, opened it, and slid the picture over to her.

She took it and a smile lit her face. It was one of his favorite pictures of the two of them together. He and Henry had gone riding that day, so long ago. Over the course of the day they'd stopped to help a lady whose car was stuck in the mud, caught and cooked fish over an open fire for lunch, and helped at Tuck's when one of his mares delivered twins. They were exhausted and filthy, and it was one of the happiest days of his life. The picture showed the two of them, each kneeling by one of the newborn colts as they were getting on their feet for the first time.

He closed his eyes as a new wave of grief rolled over him. Amazing how a picture that has always brought great happiness now brought such pain. He got up and refilled his coffee to give himself a moment to get his composure back.

"I'd like to hear the story one day."

He nodded once. "Someday. So, tell me what you're thinking."

"I was just thinking about how people grieve." She handed the picture back to him. "I treat patients all the time who are experiencing grief, among other issues. Their grief comes from all kinds of losses – jobs, friendships, security, friends and family, trust. The point is, each person grieves differently."

"Some people do it better than others?"

"Well, there's not really a right or wrong way to grieve unless what you're doing is self-destructive or hurts someone else."

"Drinking too much, making bad financial decisions, fighting…"

"Yes. You're right though, some people have better coping skills than others or a better support system. The point I was getting at is people tend to have a general way to grieve. For example, some people need to be surrounded by friends and family all the time. They always want someone to talk to, and the busier they keep themselves the better off they are. Others tend to want a lot of quiet time. They need to be alone a lot, maybe more than usual. They process grief very privately. And there are people at all points in between." She held up a finger as she finally got to her point. "But, that pattern doesn't typically change.

It stays the same no matter what the loss is."

He sat back, coffee in hand and considered what she'd told him. "Okay, that makes sense, so…?"

"So, I'm wondering why Tobias changed."

"What do you mean?"

"My grandmother died over twenty years ago. He has pictures of her everywhere, in his study, the bedroom, the living room, the walls in the hallway."

"Right?" He still hadn't made the connection.

"His only brother vanishes without a trace. He makes a statement to a reporter about how devastated the family is." She leaned in closer. "You said it yourself, there isn't a trace of Martin anywhere in this house. Not in all the papers, no letters. Nothing. Nothing to indicate Martin ever existed. Why?"

Zach sucked in a breath. He'd never considered it, but then he hadn't known about the brother until tonight. He braced himself on the counter as he considered the implications. He'd give anything to be able to talk to Henry about this. About anything. "Henry would know."

"I think Henry did know," she agreed softly. "I think that's what got him killed."

Zach scrubbed his hands over his face then pushed them through his hair. "Grace, back then Henry was the sheriff. This was a major crime committed in his county. It's not something he would have covered up."

"I'm not saying he did, Zach. We need more information before we draw any conclusions. I'm just trying to work with what I know." She was thoughtful for a moment. "Did Henry ever discuss interesting cases with you?"

He knew where she was headed this time and he didn't like it. It was the pattern thing again, and she was right. "He told me stories all the time about bad guys he chased and caught, about some that got away. He hated those."

She smiled. "I'm sure. I'm also sure there were many he didn't tell you about, for one reason or another. I'm not saying there was anything nefarious about that. He could never have told you about every case, and I'm sure there were some too troubling or inappropriate for him to talk about. You've probably had a lot like that."

He nodded and relaxed a little, then suddenly grinned. "Did you say nefarious?"

Her eyes narrowed, which might have made her look stern and angry except for the laughter dancing there. He was struck again by how pretty she was. Weird. It seemed to keep getting lost amid the other things about her he found so attractive. She had the adventurous spirit of a child and the sharp wit of someone who read people for a living. It was a heady combination. And she always smelled delicious.

He sincerely hoped she was not reading him right now. He raised an eyebrow, waiting for her answer.

"As a matter of fact, I did say that. It's an appropriate word for the situation."

That was her teacher voice. Prim and proper and he loved it, not that he would ever tell her that.

"And," she continued, "I just like saying it."

They both laughed and it felt good to let go of the tension of the evening.

She pulled one leg up, wrapping her arms around it for support. "Thanks for coming tonight, Zach. I know it probably could have waited until tomorrow, but I'm not sure I could have slept without talking to someone. I knew you'd understand."

"I'm glad you called. I want you to any time. We'll figure it out, Grace. We already know more than we did a day ago. We'll keep finding pieces until everything makes sense."

The earlier tension gone, fatigue hit him like a wrecking ball. He walked to her side of the island, took her hand and pulled her to her feet. They walked to the front door together. He kept hold of her hand, and lifted his other hand to stroke back the hair from her face. He met and held her gaze for a long moment, brushing her cheek softly with his thumb. She stood still, never breaking eye contact. Temptation on two pretty feet. *Soon.*

He lifted her hand and kissed it gently. "Goodnight, Grace. Sleep well."

He drove slowly back to town, his mind racing with everything he'd learned tonight. Hopefully Grace would sleep well, because he was pretty sure he wouldn't sleep at all.

Chapter Twenty-One

Zach was at his desk early working on a game plan for following up on his conversation with Grace. Someone knocked and he looked up from making some notes as Ross pushed through the door.

"Whoa, boss. Here." Ross offered coffee. "You look like you need this more than me, and I need it bad." He dropped into a chair across from Zach. "What's up?"

Zach grabbed the cup like a drowning man grabbing a life raft and drank deeply. He saw Ross wince. It was hot. He didn't care.

"I can see about getting that in I.V. form if you think it'd help?"

Zach shook his head. "Couldn't hurt."

Ross frowned. "Did I miss something last night? I didn't get any calls."

"Nothing official." Zach took him through the evening, explaining what Grace had found.

Ross was stunned. "So you're both left wondering what, if anything, your grandfathers knew?"

"That's the gist of it, yeah. Right now I don't know whether to miss Henry or fantasize about punching him. Tuck, too."

"Makes you wonder who else knows something. Five people missing? Everyone would have been talking about that, wondering who would be next." He shook his head. "So what's your plan?"

"I'm going to start interviewing anyone who was here back then. See what pops up. Someone has to know something."

Ross nodded. "I was just thinking the same thing. Mind if I help?"

"It's still not an official investigation."

"I'm aware. You haven't heard anything from the state guys yet, have you?"

"Nothing beyond the obligatory 'this is top priority'. I think they're stumped and don't want to admit it. I was expecting more for the murder of a former sheriff." He didn't need to see Ross' expression to know he sounded bitter.

"Yeah, me too. So where do you want to start?"

Zach's expression hardened. "With that smarmy little weasel who almost got himself shot last week."

Ross grinned. "She was pretty impressive, wasn't she?"

Zach nodded, smiling in return. "She was. I think she really would have shot him."

"Pretty sure you're right about that. I wouldn't want to be facing her down when she's mad at me." He smirked at Zach. "Might be something to keep in mind, buddy."

Zach leaned back in his chair. "Might be important at that."

Ross turned serious. "I could take a run at some of the old timers for you."

"Fine. I'll be glad to have the help, but the weasel is mine."

* * *

Zach pushed open the door just as the weasel was coming to lock up for lunch. He knew Forsythe's secretary went to lunch every day at eleven forty-five on the nose. It was the perfect time for a private chat.

Forsythe stepped back, surprised, and Zach caught a flicker of fear before Forsythe could compose himself.

"Forsythe, glad I caught you. Got a minute?"

"Zachariah, I was just closing up for lunch. Can we schedule something later in the week?"

140

Zach smiled the smile he used on suspects to put them at ease - right before he pounced. "It's important. Won't take but a minute." He closed the door. "Let me lock up for you so we don't get interrupted. You never know who's going to walk in, do you?"

He made it point to flick the lock quickly. It made a loud click.

The little flicker of fear was there again, just for a moment, but it was enough. Zach held out his hand toward Forsythe's office. "Shall we sit? Might as well be comfortable."

Forsythe pulled himself together and inclined his head toward Zach. "Of course. Please come in." So very civil. He seated himself behind his big desk as if it were a shield and he was under attack.

Zach made no effort to put him at ease.

"Now, what can I do for you, Zachariah?"

"Tell me about the five men who disappeared from Cullen County forty years ago."

Forsythe placed both hands on his desk and studied them as if searching through memories to the time of the disappearances. It would have been an effective ploy, but Zach was watching and caught the sharp intake of breath and the involuntary widening of the eyes Forsythe couldn't control. A direct hit.

Forsythe lifted his head, a puzzled frown on his face. "That was a lifetime ago, Sheriff. I remember in general, of course, it was such a major tragedy for this town. I'm afraid I can't remember many details, though. Why do you ask?"

Zach shrugged casually. "I've been looking over some cold cases and this one caught my attention. I'd never heard about it, and of course it made me curious when I saw that one of the men who disappeared was Martin Tucker."

"Hmm. Yes, now that you mention it, I do recall that."

"Funny how you can know someone your whole life and never know such an important detail. I never knew Tuck had a brother, or any family except his wife, for that matter." He sat back, shaking his head. "I just can't get over that."

Forsythe nodded vigorously. "Yes, yes, it's not something too many would remember, I expect. It was a long time ago."

"It was," Zach agreed, congenially. "What can you tell me about that time or those men? Since you were Tuck's lawyer I thought maybe he'd talked to you about it."

Forsythe's expression morphed from guarded to sly. He drew a deep breath, sat back in his huge chair and smiled his snake-oil-salesman smile. "I'm sorry, Zachariah. I'd truly like to help you, but I'm sure you understand that anything Tobias and I discussed was and still is privileged. I'm afraid I can't help you at all."

Zach nodded. "Not asking for anything confidential. What can you tell me about the other families?"

"Nothing. Nothing at all. They were represented by other attorneys." He sighed dramatically. "It was a terrible time for this town, Sheriff. Tobias was very worried about his brother. The whole town was on edge as you might imagine. Martin Tucker was the last to go missing, but it was months before people stopped being so scared. Tobias was the only one to stay. The other four families moved away and everyone eventually stopped talking about it." He shook he head and managed to look sorrowful. "It's one of those cold cases that will never be solved."

Zach stayed silent, eyes locked with the weasel. Finally, he stood to leave.

The weasel looked relieved.

"Don't be too sure about that, Forsythe. Don't you watch the news? Cold cases are getting solved all the time. Thanks for your time. You've helped me more than you know."

Zach enjoyed the last flicker of fear as he left the office. "Don't forget to lock up, now," he called from the front door. His smile disappeared as he headed for his car. Forsythe was in it up to his beady little weasel eyes.

* * *

Forsythe sank back into his big leather chair and gripped the arms to keep his hands from shaking. He stared at the doorway half expecting the sheriff to come back.

The man who entered was not the sheriff, nor was he making any effort to pretend he wasn't angry.

"He knows!" He hovered over the desk and glared at Forsythe before pacing the length of the office.

He was right. Forsythe had looked into the sheriff's eyes and seen the knowledge there despite his cordial presentation. Somehow, he'd learned what happened all those years ago. But he didn't know everything. Only two people left alive knew the whole truth and they were both in this room. He glanced at the man continuing to pace with quick, angry steps.

A ribbon of fear snaked through him, twisting his stomach into knots and his heart like a painful, breath-stealing fist in his chest. In all the years since the disappearances he'd never known fear of exposure like he did at this moment. The man was almost twenty years younger than Forsythe, but he was his greatest threat. If pushed, this man would tell everything and take Forsythe down with him in a spectacularly public fashion. Cornered animals were particularly vicious. The only question now was which animal would strike first.

As if reading Forsythe's thoughts, the man abruptly stopped pacing and pointed a finger right at him. "I told you killing them was a mistake," he hissed.

"I'm not the one who killed them." Forsythe was scared, but he wasn't going down without a fight. "You would do well to remember that."

The man's eyes narrowed ever more, crimson staining his angry face.

Forsythe fleetingly wished the man would have a heart attack or stroke. That would solve a lot of problems. It would create others - like getting rid of the body - but he had enough shady clients to handle that.

"Is that a threat, Forsythe?"

"Not at all. Just a reminder that we're in this together, like it or not. There's nothing to worry about unless someone starts talking. They have old information and suspicions. That's all. Be sure you don't give them more than that."

The man sank into a chair and sneered at Forsythe. "They're about to have a lot more than that. I hope you're ready with an explanation because you're gonna need it."

Forsythe shook his head and frowned. "What on earth are you talking about?"

The man leaned in close. Too close. "They went to the bunker yesterday. I think they plan to open it."

Cold flashed through him and a giant suction pulled air from his lungs. The room spun. He pushed back from his desk and lowered his head between his knees, desperately needing to return the blood flow that had deserted his brain. His vision narrowed and he fought the blackness.

His chest burned with the effort to breathe. When he could sit up he reached into his pocket and pulled out the nitroglycerin pills he rarely used anymore. He put one under his tongue and lowered his head to the desk. He was afraid he might die right there. Then he thought about what would happen if he were exposed. Death might not be so bad after all.

He took another pill before the squeezing in his chest eased off. Now it felt like the top of his head would blow off. The nitro always did that. He collapsed back into his chair utterly spent. Sweat covered his body, making his clothes and hair stick to him.

He stared at the man still sitting across from him. During the entire terrifying episode he had not moved from the chair. He wore a slight smile as if he'd enjoyed the show. Maybe he'd hope to see

Forsythe die. Maybe he was thinking about liabilities, too.

The man whistled softly. "Whew. That was a close call."

Forsythe's anger flared at the mocking tone.

"I thought you might check out on me before I could ask for advice from my lawyer." His airy laugh turned into a gurgling wheeze, then a full-blown cough. He slapped the arm of the chair, amused at himself.

Forsythe needed to go home. He wasn't certain he could walk. "You need to leave. My secretary will be back from lunch soon and I have appointments. You can't be seen here."

"What about our little problem?"

"I'll handle it. Now leave!"

"I could take care of it for you. For us."

"No!" Forsythe shouted, angry, and afraid. "No more killing! Enough, do you hear me? I said I'll take care of it and I will." He leaned over the desk to glare at the man. "Get out! Now!"

The man backed toward the door, hands up in surrender. "Leaving. Don't worry though, I'm never far away." He turned and disappeared from the office.

Forsythe heard the front door open when his secretary returned from lunch. As was her habit, she stuck her head in to tell him she was back. She frowned when she saw him. He could only imagine what he looked like.

"Anything you need, sir?"

"Something has come up that I need to take care of this afternoon. Would you please cancel my appointments? I'll be leaving in a few minutes."

"Sure thing. Want me to call if anything comes in?"

"No, just save it for tomorrow. I'm sure it won't be anything that can't wait."

"I'll take care of it. Have a good afternoon, boss."

"Thank you, Ann. You too. Please close the door on your way

out."

He reached for the water pitcher on his desk, poured a glass and sank back in his chair. He gulped the water like a dying man in the desert. How did the sheriff know? There wasn't a single reference to the disappearances anywhere in town. He'd personally taken care of every back issue of the newspaper from that time. The families of the men had moved away after years, unable to remain in a place with so many bad memories. It was way before the sheriff's time. No one talked about it anymore.

Grace must have found something. It was the only explanation. Tuck had kept something in writing and she'd found it and told Zachariah.

He closed his eyes, disgust, frustration, and regret settling in his gut. He hadn't had time to get to anything the night he went to Tobias's house and almost got shot. Panic threatened to overwhelm him. If the sheriff knew about the missing men, did he also now know what had happened to them? No. If that had been the case he'd be sitting in jail now.

The sheriff didn't know everything. Forsythe had one last chance to save himself. If he failed he would be as good as dead. It might not be too late yet, but if they opened that bunker...

He whirled around and threw his glass against the wall, shattering it to pieces. He left by his private entrance not caring at all what his secretary would think.

Chapter Twenty-Two

Ross strolled into the diner pleased to see Zach waiting for him at a quiet table in the back. The dinner rush was over and he needed some uninterrupted time with his boss. He ordered a Reuben and a sweet tea and dug in when it arrived.

Zach sported a well-established five-o'clock shadow to go with the dark smudges under his eyes. The table might have been the only thing holding him up. Rough was an understatement.

"You look like death warmed over, buddy," Ross said around a big bite of sandwich. "Last night catching up with you?"

"Yeah." He took a large swig of coffee that had no hope of helping him now. "I figure you've got about fifteen minutes to say what you need to say. Then I'm done."

Ross swallowed, wiped his mouth and picked up the folder he'd brought with him. He pushed the plate away to make room and opened it to scan the pages inside. "Well, it's more what I didn't find than what I did."

He glanced up at Zach and figured he had more like five minutes. "I managed to track down three of the families of the missing men and speak to them." He grimaced. "I opened some old wounds. Hate that."

"And?"

"Well, first let me say that I tried to track down the case files on all of those men." He paused to be sure he had Zach's full attention. "They're missing."

Zach's focus got laser sharp. "All of them? No trace? Not even a partial file?"

"Not a single scrap of paper. Quite a coincidence, huh?"

"I don't believe in coincidences."

"Neither do I. So, next I checked the newspaper office. I looked through every box that had a date even close – and can I just say how disgusting that was?"

"Been there, done that."

"Yeah, well, it was all for nothing. I couldn't find anything."

Zach shook his head. "I didn't find anything either. More coincidence?"

Ross snorted. "Yeah, man-made coincidence I think."

"Forsythe."

Ross cocked an eyebrow in question. "What do you know?"

"I went to see him earlier today. I asked point blank about the disappearances. He looked like he was about to stroke out. He knows something. Maybe everything."

"Couldn't get him to talk?"

"He wrapped himself in attorney-client privilege. He wishes he could help, yada, yada, yada." His expression hardened. "I'm trying not to get paranoid about what Tuck knew or why he needs to be protected."

Ross sat back and drank his tea while he considered that. Tuck's brother had been the last to disappear. Soon after that, Forsythe became Tuck's lawyer and had been ever since.   The meeting with Grace, breaking in to steal papers. It was all related, but he had no clue how.

"I wish I could explain it. I've never liked Forsythe. He's too—"

Zach smirked. "Smarmy? That's what Grace calls him. I think she's right."

"She's a smart lady. Maybe we'll get to meet on better terms next time, like when she's not holding a gun."

They laughed, but Zach was fading fast and Ross knew he didn't have much time left. He grabbed another quick bite. "Here's the plan. I'm going to try to contact the other family tomorrow and interview them. I'm also going to check with the state guys to see where things stand. Then I'm going to see if I can get a look at some financial records. Will you give me permission to look at Henry's bank records?"

Zach nodded. "I'll call Rick in the morning and okay it, and sign whatever they need." He rubbed his eyes and groaned. "I'm sure I should be able to think of this, but what are you looking for?"

"Not sure yet. I'm hoping I'll know it when I see it." He paused. "I'd like to look at Tuck's history as well. You think she'll give me permission?"

Zach shrugged. "I can't speak for her, but I know she wants answers as much as we do. I think she'll be open to it. Give her a call. Tell her you're looking at Henry's stuff, too."

"I'll do that."

"Anything else?"

"Yeah, but it can wait. You need to get home before you fall on your face. Want me to drive you?"

Zach made a rude gesture and Ross laughed. "Fine, but I'm following you so I can lay on the horn when you start swerving."

He left money on the table and they headed out. Ross followed Zach despite his protests, then headed home himself. He had some things to go over before he could sleep, not the least of which was assessing the danger his friend was in. Someone had poked a sleeping bear. He had the worst feeling that bear was about to come roaring to life and savage whoever was in its path. He was determined to see that it wasn't Zach Wells.

* * *

"Grace, it's Ross Taylor from the sheriff's department. We met the other night."

"I remember, Officer Taylor. How are you?"

"Fine, thanks, and make it Ross, okay?"

"Ross, then. Is something wrong?"

"No, but I have a favor to ask."

A pause. "Okay."

"We're looking into the backgrounds of the missing men, trying to find some connection that might help us figure out what happened, and how this might be connected to Tuck and Henry. One thing we need to check for is some kind of financial connection. Zach has given me permission to look into Henry's financial history. I'd like your permission to check Tobias's. There's no court order or anything like that. We don't have anything to support that, so it would be strictly voluntary. I know it's your business now—"

"Do it." She didn't hesitate for one moment. "I haven't touched anything in his accounts yet. Everything is just as he left it, except Forsythe no longer has access to anything. I'll call the bank or give you something in writing. Whatever you need. When do you want to start?"

He took an easy breath. "Tomorrow, if that's no trouble. I'm sure the bank will want something notarized."

"No problem. I'll type out something tonight and be there when the bank opens in the morning. You can start right after that." She was silent for a moment. "I have one condition."

The tension started to creep back. "Which is?"

"I want to know whatever you find, as soon as you find it."

He considered the request. It was a difficult promise to make when he had no clue what he would find.

"I don't care how bad it is, Ross. I'm already wondering some not so great things. I need to know the truth, one way or the other. That's my offer."

"Fair enough. I'll keep you informed. Whatever I find you'll know about, good, bad, or ugly."

"Thank you."

Ross hoped she'd be as grateful if the news was bad. She'd had high hopes when she met Tobias. The inheritance he'd left her had already begun to tarnish along with her perception of her grandfather. Ross had a bad feeling that before the investigation was over, Grace's vision for a family would be left a battered, bloody mess.

Chapter Twenty-Three

"You know what to do?" Forsythe wasn't taking any chances.

The man laughed a gravelly, sinister laugh that chilled Forsythe to the bone. Every fiber of his being mistrusted this man. They had kept one another's secrets in a delicate truce that had nothing to do with trust, and everything to do with fear of exposure. Both for very different reasons.

He was out of options and totally in survival mode. He couldn't remember the last time his pulse had kept a steady, comfortable beat, or when he had not worked for every breath. Eating was impossible. He tried to take another deep breath to settle the nausea, but his chest and belly were constricted like a debutante in a corset. He might not ever breathe right again.

He shook with fury and more than a little fear. The more precarious their situation became the cockier his partner got. He was a loose cannon. If they got through this alive Forsythe would take great pleasure in killing him. He'd made provisions to leave the country and disappear forever, but he couldn't afford to leave this kind of a loose end. The risk was too great, and the man's sanity questionable. Forsythe eyed the man staring back at him and wondered if there were two murders being plotted in this room. The corset cinched another notch tighter.

The man sneered at him. "This ain't my first rodeo." He stood and stretched, walked to the door where he turned and pointed a finger at Forsythe. "You just make sure you have your end covered. And don't get any stupid ideas about setting me up. I know where the bodies are buried." He leaned in. "And I know which closet you keep your skeletons in."

He slammed the door and Forsythe felt it like a bullet. What had he done? Why had he ever thought they could get away with this? He'd never felt remorse, but he'd often felt fear. Never more than now. There would be no explaining things away, no justification. The town would turn on him like a pack of wolves. His sins were many and big. He tried not to think of how many more would be added to his account before he could make his escape.

* * *

Visions of a big country breakfast tantalized and teased as Grace drove into town Friday morning. She planned to be at the bank when it opened at nine, which gave her just enough time to stop at the diner for breakfast. She held her breath for a moment then let it out slowly. The food would be welcome, she wasn't so sure about the people. In the two weeks she'd been here, she'd been in town three times, two of those times for funerals.

An outsider. That's what she was. The gossip mill had to be working overtime. People loved to talk. She rolled her eyes. She'd come to town. Tobias was killed. She got rich.

Please! I'd be talkin' too!"

She punched a button on her console and her favorite gospel music pealed from the speakers. Her most recent prayers had been so simple, prayers for wisdom and direction. One day at a time. Many times in her life during the most trying times, her prayers had simply been for God to hang on to her and not let go. So it was now. She drove on toward town as the peace and message of the music soothed her soul like a soft caress.

She was almost to the city limits when her phone rang. The

number wasn't familiar but she answered anyway.

"Hello?"

"Uh, Ms. Tucker?"

"Yes, this is Grace."

"Oh, good. Um, this is Lou Ann Simmons from the newspaper office in town? We haven't met yet, but I was a friend of your granddaddy's. I'm sure sorry about what happened." She sounded rushed and a bit breathless.

"Thank you, Lou Ann. I appreciate that. Is there something I can do for you?"

"What? Oh no, no, I just, uh, I found some old articles about Tuck, uh, your granddaddy, and thought you might like to see them. I know you didn't have much time to get to know him."

Profoundly touched by the offer, Grace needed a moment to respond. "That's so thoughtful of you, thank you, and yes, I'd love to see them. I'm almost to town now. I'll stop by today and get them if that's all right?"

"Um, well, that's the thing, see I have to leave in about thirty minutes and I'll be gone the rest of the day. If you want them today you need to come by before nine."

Grace frowned. *Weird.* "Okay, why don't I come right now? I'm just a few minutes out. Will that work?"

"Sure. That's fine."

A dial tone signaled the end of the call. Grace shrugged. That was abrupt and strange. Probably not the last encounter like that.

She drove into town and took the last parking space in front of the newspaper office. Nestled between an office supply store and a pharmacy, the little office was inviting with its large glass front and pots of annuals framing the doorway. Grace pushed through the door that read, *Cullen County Times, Davis R. Wright, Owner and Managing Editor.* Office hours and emergency contact numbers were listed beneath the name. A bell jingled at her entrance as a woman emerged

154

from a back room.

The woman wore a denim skirt and a pale pink cardigan. Teased, bottle-blond hair added a good four inches to her medium height. Too much makeup did nothing to hide the ravages of years of cigarettes and sun. Eye shadow, the blue of every pre-teen girl learning to use makeup, vied for attention with bubblegum pink lipstick on pursed lips.

Grace guessed the woman had never been out of Cullen County. Her gaze landed on an employee badge with *Lou Ann* etched on it. She smiled at the woman, grateful for her efforts to find information about Tobias, and did her best not to jump to conclusions.

"Lou Ann? I'm Grace Tucker. I'm so glad you called. I can't tell you how much it means to me to learn something about To— about my grandfather."

Lou Ann's gaze never quite met hers. Grace worked hard to banish the thought that the woman didn't like her. A person didn't go out of their way to do something like this for someone they didn't like.

Lou Ann busied herself straightening the desk. "I've got the copies for you in a folder."

"Thanks. I'd like to read them while I have breakfast. Oh, and I want to pay you for them. How much do I owe you?"

She looked puzzled and shook her head. "No charge. It's on the house. They're downstairs in the archives. On the table." She gestured vaguely toward the stairs. "I need to make a phone call. You'll have to get them yourself." She abruptly turned her back on Grace and picked up the phone.

Grace stared at her back for a moment, rolled her eyes and headed for the stairs. She flipped the switch at the top, and light flooded the stairwell and the room below. Halfway down, the musty smell reached her, and dust tickled her nose and throat. The stairway was narrow and steep and she gratefully stepped off the bottom step into the archive room.

The wall to the left contained shelves of bound volumes of papers. The rest of the room was worse than Tobias's attic. Boxes stacked four and five high leaned precariously in columns all around the room. Some were crushed, others showed signs of water damage. An odor of cigarettes pervaded the space and Grace shuddered at the thought of what might be scurrying around down here.

She spotted a card table on the far end of the room with what she hoped was her folder on top. Turning sideways, she squeezed her way through the pig trail that ran through the stacks and finally made her way to the table. She glanced down at herself and grimaced at the dust and grime clinging to her clothes and even her hair. Several vigorous swats produced little more than tiny dust clouds that added to the stuff already floating in the air.

She groaned, resigned to spending the entire day in town covered in dust and who knew what else. *You're gonna make a great impression, Grace.* She reached for the folder. A scuffling sound startled her and she froze, looking around for the creature making that noise, and praying it wasn't close to her. She didn't see anything and reached for the folder again. There was that noise again, this time from higher up. Her peripheral vision caught a fleeting glimpse of a shadow. A man-sized shadow. Adrenaline shot through her. Her breath caught as she raised her arms protectively, but it was too late.

Arms like bands of steel wrapped around her from behind, locking her arms to her side and preventing her from fighting. She screamed. One huge hand covered her mouth and nose with a cloth. She smelled the sickening, sweet smell of chloroform and full-blown panic set in. She fought with everything in her, kicking and squirming. Anything to get away from that smell. Too late she realized that her rapid, panicked breathing was only hastening the delivery of the drug to her system. She tried to stop and hold her breath, but it was too late. The world became fuzzy and narrowed to pinholes of light. Then it was gone.

Chapter Twenty-Four

Zach emerged from a long, hot shower and headed to the kitchen to scrounge for breakfast. A knock on the door had him detouring through the living room, empty coffee mug in hand. Pastor Andy Clary grinned at him over a bag from the local bakery.

"If those are donuts, what took you so long?"

Andy laughed. "Marriage counseling. At seven in the morning, can you believe it?"

"Come on in." Zach stepped back to give him room. "Tom and Allison?"

"Yep. Wedding's in two weeks."

Zach held up a mug and Andy nodded. "How's everyone holding up?"

"About like you'd expect with two controlling mothers who don't like each other or their child's chosen mate." He accepted the coffee with a contented sigh. "Perfect."

Zach snagged a donut from the crumpled bag on the coffee table. "Have you suggested eloping?"

Andy snorted. "Every time we meet. No such luck." He grinned. "We may need a few of your deputies for the big day."

"Crowd control?"

"Mother control. It ain't gonna be pretty."

"We're here to serve."

"'Preciate it." Andy stretched out his legs and balanced his coffee on his belly with one hand, a donut in the other.

"Drove by Henry's place on the way out today. Looks good. You doing double duty keeping the place up?"

Zach rolled his eyes. "Hardly. I've been out a few times since…" He rolled his shoulders and took another long drink of coffee. "Henry's got a good crew. Most of them have been with him close to twenty years. They all wanted to stay on. They keep their jobs and I don't have to worry about the place for now. It works for everyone."

"Long term?"

"Not a clue. I haven't really had time to think about it."

Andy nodded, solemnly. "How's the investigation coming?"

"Some things are starting to come together." He glanced apologetically at Andy. "Nothing I can talk about yet. Sorry."

Andy held up a hand. "No problem. Good to hear you're making some progress. Anything I can do?"

Zach shrugged. "Pray?"

"I can do that. Anything else?"

"No, but thanks for asking, man. It means a lot."

Andy sat back in his chair. "Can I ask you a personal question?"

Zach held his gaze for a moment. "You can ask."

"When was the last time *you* prayed?"

Zach shook his head. "God doesn't want to hear from me, Andy. I've given him no reason to listen to me, much less answer a prayer."

"I see."

"What does that mean?"

"What do *you* mean?"

"I haven't been to church in weeks."

"Months."

"Fine. Months."

"And?"

Zach blew out a long breath and pushed a hand through his hair. "And along with everything else, I'm finding out some things about my family that don't exactly put me in a position to ask for anything."

Andy was silent for a moment, then took a big swig of coffee. "So, when was the last time you think you had a right to pray?"

Zach's eyes narrowed. He could see where Andy was headed with his questions, sort of. "It's not that simple."

"Really? You grew up in church, Zach. Did you pay attention at all?"

Now that was uncalled for. So much for a friendly visit.

"Of course I did, but it doesn't change how things are now."

Andy shook his head and looked at Zach like he was a slow child. "It should change everything, Zach. You're talking like you have to earn the right to pray - as if that could ever happen. And just in case you've forgotten that part, it could not. You feel like you've moved away from God. Maybe you have. It happens to all of us at one time or another. Maybe he's using this situation to move you back. Have to pray to do that."

"There are things you don't know yet, Andy. Things I can't talk about." He shook his head as sadness and shame overwhelmed him. "People have been hurt and I can't fix it."

"Are you responsible for it? And by that I mean, did you do the hurting?"

Zach shook his head.

"Then your responsibility is not to fix it, is it? Maybe in your position as sheriff your job is to bring justice and closure to the situation. If I were you I wouldn't want to try doing that without God's help."

"The day of Henry's funeral," Zach said softly.

"What?"

"I prayed that day. First time in a long time. I just didn't know what else to do. Grace and I've talked about it, too."

"Grace. Tobias's granddaughter?"

Zach nodded. "Some coincidence, huh?"

Andy shook his head. "Nope. No coincidences with God. He

was getting you ready for this conversation." He stood to leave. "Zach, look, I'm not saying use God like a magic wand, just pulling him out when you need him. The fact is you need him every day. We all do. Whatever's going on here is big and if anything in your life needs prayer right now, this is probably it. If you wait 'til you earn the right then you'll never pray again. God knows what you need. He could fix it with a thought if he wanted to, but he wants you to talk to him. So, just do it. Start a conversation and see where it goes."

"I do a lot of praying for you, Zach. It's probably what saves your sorry hide on the job." He grinned, then grew serious again. "The least you can do is pray for yourself. If you won't even do that…" He shrugged and pulled open the door. "Call me if you need me. I'll be around."

The least you could do is pray for yourself.

Zach's gaze rested on his Bible sitting on the coffee table. He picked it up and opened it to the place marked with a bulletin. He glanced at the date. Six months ago. Had it really been that long since he'd been in church? Read his Bible? Prayed? He remembered the sermon for that day from Psalm 46. Andy had preached it the Sunday after two high school kids had been killed in an alcohol-related crash. The devastated congregation had needed some words of hope. Just like he did now. He sat back and read the words again.

God is our refuge and strength,
an ever-present help in trouble.
Therefore we will not fear…

Zach rested the open Bible on his chest and leaned his head back, eyes closed. *I have no idea how to do this anymore, God. It's been a long time. I'm sorry about that. Especially now when so much is on the line. I need to find some answers and I need to know how in the world I'm supposed to live with what I find. It's already bad and I'm afraid it's going to be so much worse when I know everything. I want to do better. Help me to find the answers I need and to know what to do.*

* * *

Ross got a coffee to go and left the diner headed for the bank. He greeted the manager and explained the purpose for his visit, then sat to read the paper and wait. After thirty minutes he called Grace's cell. It went straight to voice mail. He went back to the paper for another fifteen minutes then called again and left a message that he was going back to the station and for her to call him when she got to town.

He made his way through the bullpen to his office trying to tamp down his frustration. He hated wasting time, and he was anxious to get a look at those records. He frowned. Grace had been eager for him to check things out, almost insistent. Had she changed her mind?

He opened a folder to find his list of names and numbers for the families he needed to talk to. By the time Zach got to the office he'd spoken to two of them.

"Thought you'd be at the bank."

Ross shifted in his chair and stretched to work out some kinks. "I was, for an hour. Grace never showed and I needed to make some calls. Have you talked to her today?"

Zach frowned. "No. Did you try to call her?"

"Twice. Left a message both times. Told her to give me a call when she's ready to go."

Before he finished speaking, Zach pulled out his phone and dialed her number by heart. Ross smirked at him, and was ignored.

"Grace, it's Zach. Call me when you get this. Just wanted to be sure you're okay. Ross is available to go to the bank whenever you're ready. Call me."

Ross watched Zach pocket his phone, concern on his face.

"You looking for Grace Tucker?"

They turned together to see the waitress from the diner standing outside Ross' office.

"Gina, what are you doing here?"

"Had to get fingerprinted for my carry permit." She grinned. "I'm gettin' a gun for my birthday."

"I'm trying not to think about that," Ross said, wryly.

She laughed. "So you're looking for Tuck's granddaughter?"

"Have you seen her?"

"Sure, just this morning. She was going into the newspaper office."

Zach frowned. "What time was that?"

"Just about eight. I was in the office supply place getting some stuff for my boss. I came out as she was going in." She looked curious now. "Everything okay?"

Ross needed to get her out fast. "Everything's fine, just a little miscommunication. Nothing to worry about." He gently took her arm and led her to the hallway. "I appreciate the information, Gina. Tell Don hello for me."

She winked like she knew he was trying to get rid of her. "I'll do that. You all have a good day now."

Ross looked at Zach. "You want to call?"

"Nope," he answered as he headed for the door. "I want to go."

"Right behind you, boss."

Chapter Twenty-Five

Zach pushed his way through the door making it bang on the wall behind him as he entered the newspaper office. Lou Ann looked up from her magazine, startled by the noise, and probably his presence. Beneath that pancake makeup the color drained from her face. A hard knot of cold fear settled into Zack's gut. She was guilty of something, and it wasn't going to be good.

"Mornin', Lou Ann."

"Sheriff. What can I do for you?"

"You can tell me what Grace Tucker was doing here this morning."

She was going to lie. Her gaze shifted away from him and she ducked her head. A muscle ticked in his jaw. He didn't have time for games, the sense of unease growing with every passing moment.

"I know she was here, Lou Ann. People saw her. What was she doing here?"

"Nothing. She was just picking up copies of some articles about Tuck." She frowned at him, then got busy folding papers and meticulously going over the creases.

"You made the copies?"

She nodded.

"How long was she here?"

He caught her quick glance toward the stairs. "She went down there?"

She shrugged and frowned at him again. "She's not here, Sheriff. She left when she got her copies, I told you."

Zach headed around the desk to the stairwell. "That's not what I asked you. Did she go downstairs?"

Lou Ann stared at him, trembling like a rabbit caught in a trap.

Zach looked at Ross. "Bring her." He started down the stairs flipping the light switch as he went. At the bottom of the stairs he stopped to take in the scene. The place was a disaster, especially the far-right corner by the table. Boxes were overturned and knocked down and the table was shoved all the way against the wall. There had been a struggle here recently. Grace and who else?

Ross pointed Lou Ann to a chair. "Stay." He turned to help Zach examine the area for some indication of who had been here. They inspected the floor around the table and the stacks of boxes close by.

Tucked against the side of a large box Zach found a piece of material scrunched up in a ball. He pulled a pen from his front pocket and carefully lifted the cloth from the floor to examine it. As he did he caught the tiniest hint of an odor that sent adrenaline exploding through him. He held it up for Ross to see.

"Chloroform," he said tightly.

Ross swore under his breath.

Lou Ann began to cry.

* * *

The pounding pain in her head brought Grace to full awareness. Her stomach churned. The effort to open her eyes was almost more than she could muster. When she finally managed to pry one eye open, panic threatened to rob her of every bit of self-control. It was pitch black. She waited for her eyes to adjust to the dark and capture the faintest bit of light…nothing. Not the tiniest spark.

She ached all over. She tried to stretch and gasped as she realized she was shackled to a chair. She tried to move the chair but it was bolted to the floor. Her sense of the place was of a deep, dark cave.

164

It felt huge. She felt exposed.

And cold. It was so cold.

How long had she been here? She had no sense of time. More to the point, why? Who would do such a thing? She had been in the newspaper office to pick up some copies that—

Lou Ann. She'd acted weird. Had she known? She had to have. She was the one who called. Grace shook her head, then immediately regretted it. Every heartbeat pounded in her skull. Lou Ann hadn't attacked her in the archive room, and she certainly hadn't carried her here. So who?

She needed to think. She needed a plan. Would they come back? Would they just leave her here to die? Was she now the sixth disappearance?

Don't go there.

It took every ounce of willpower she had not to panic. She focused on taking slow, steady breaths. For now, she could try to get the nausea under control. Then maybe her head would ease up and she'd be able to think of something.

The cold was going to be a problem. Already it leached into her bones and she shivered, adding to her pain. Her whole body was one giant ache. She wanted to cry, but that would waste precious energy and accomplish nothing. She tried to hold herself up to relieve pressure on her wrists, but couldn't make her body obey.

I don't want to die here. God, please help me.

That was her last thought before consciousness slipped away once more.

* * *

Lou Ann sat in an interrogation room crying. She hadn't stopped since they'd been in the archive room and found evidence of a kidnapping. Rather than waste time interrogating her at the newspaper office, Zach had taken ten minutes to drive her back to the station to explain her rights and shove her in the tiny room. Ross called a deputy to guard the crime scene, and the lab techs to gather evidence. As soon as they were on scene he joined Zach at the station. An APB was out and every cop in the county was looking for Grace.

Zach pushed open the interrogation room door, startling Lou Ann into silence. He stood across from her not caring that his body language and his expression scared her to the point of speechlessness. He also didn't care that his personal interest in Grace made it inappropriate for him to question Lou Ann.

He slapped a notepad and pen onto the table, spun a chair around and straddled it. Ross entered and took up a spot close to one corner, out of the way, but close enough.

"I don't have to tell you you're in a world of trouble." He hoped he could scare her into talking. Fast. Time was wasting. "If you want any chance of not spending the rest of your life in prison you will start talking and tell me everything. Right now."

She started crying again, rocking back and forth and gulping for air between sobs. "I'm sorry. I'm so sorry. I didn't want to do it. He made me. He made me."

Zach slapped his hand hard on the table. She jumped and cried out, surprised into silence again, staring at Zach with huge, scared eyes. Behind her, Ross shifted his weight, but stayed where he was.

"Enough crying. I'm going to assume for now that Grace is alive. You help me find her – alive – and I'll talk to the D.A. for you."

She started to whimper again but a hard look from Zach stopped her and she made a visible effort to get control of herself. "I'll try. I promise."

"Start at the beginning."

She looked at him as if she didn't understand the question.

"You didn't make copies of anything, did you? That was a lie?"

She hung her head. "No."

"Why did she think you did?"

"I called her. He told me to call her and get her to the office."

Never had an interrogation moved at such a slow pace. His hands itched with the need to grab Lou Ann and shake her until she told him every secret she was hiding. He leaned forward to get in her face.

"He, who?" His voice was low and menacing. His stare did not waver from her face.

"Mr. Forsythe. He made me do it. I'm so sorry."

Zach leaned back and dropped his head for a moment. "Remington Forsythe." He locked eyes with Ross who nodded once and left the room.

Across from him, Lou Ann was crying again. Zach shook his head in disgust. What would normally have evoked sympathy now only fueled his anger. He reined it in and tried to keep his mind on the ultimate goal – finding Grace and getting her back safely.

He forced himself to move back and give Lou Ann some space. How was she connected to Forsythe? She was certainly no match for him, and Zack could imagine more than a few scenarios that ended with Lou Ann doing something illegal to save herself from Forsythe's machinations.

He slid a box of tissues in front of her. "Here."

She sniffled and pulled three tissues free to crumple them in her hand. "I'm so sorry," she whispered again. She made no eye contact now.

"Then help me."

She blew her nose and sniffled again. Nodded.

"What does Forsythe have on you to make you do something like this?"

Her face crumpled, shoulders sagged. She silently shook her head.

"Lou Ann, look at me." An order.

She looked up, made eye contact briefly, then looked down

again. A deep blush replaced the pale, scared look of a moment ago.

"You can tell me now, and I can do my best to be discreet, or you can make me dig and it all comes out in the open."

She made a small sound of distress and Zach forced himself not to be swayed by sympathy. "What's it going to be, Lou Ann?"

For one maddening moment she didn't respond. Then she bowed her head in resignation. He had her.

"He knows something about me. Something so bad…he threatened to tell people if I didn't help him." She shook her head, still staring at the table. "I knew he would do it. He's a very bad man."

"No argument there." Zach tried to encourage her now that she was cooperating. "Tell me, Lou Ann. Just spit it out. It won't get any easier."

"I had an abortion two years ago." She whispered the confession so softly he almost didn't hear. But he had heard and now anger flared in him. Not at her, but at the man who would take advantage of her, or any woman, and use a traumatic, painful experience against her.

"How is Forsythe involved in that?"

She sat back now, quieter now that the secret was out. Drained and exhausted. "The father didn't want anything to do with the baby, or me for that matter. He was worried that the whole thing would ruin his reputation." She took a deep breath. "And his marriage."

Zach stayed silent.

"Forsythe gave me money from him and I went to a clinic out of town. He said he would keep my secret, but I'd have to do some things for him from time to time."

"What kind of things?"

She shrugged. "I delivered some packages for him once."

"What was in them?"

"I don't know. I just delivered them, mostly to places out of town." She twisted her fingers together on the table. "The last thing I did was get rid of anything in the archives that mentioned those men who disappeared."

"Did you know he was going to kidnap Grace?"

"No!" She looked shocked, then ashamed. "I should have known he was planning something bad. I just never thought he would hurt her."

Zach's breath caught. "Did he hurt her?"

She shrank back from the anger in his voice. Tears welled up in her eyes, but she held his gaze. "I don't know." She shook her head quickly. "I don't think so. I heard them struggling but I never saw her after she went downstairs."

"Forsythe was waiting for her downstairs?"

She shook her head and frowned. "No, I—"

"What?"

"I don't know who was down there." She looked genuinely puzzled. "No one came in this morning except her."

"Someone was there, Lou Ann. Who else?"

She kept shaking her head.

"Who came up after that?"

"No one." At Zach's incredulous look she continued. "I opened at eight-thirty like always. No one was there and no one came until Grace. The next person to come in was you. That's it. I swear."

Zach stared at her for a long moment. Then got up and headed for the door.

"Can I go now?"

He shook his head. "Make yourself comfortable, Lou Ann. You'll be here for a while."

Zach pulled out his phone and called Ross for an update. He was waiting to talk to the judge about search warrants for Forsythe's home and office. Ross and their investigator would handle that as soon as they had ink on the warrants.

The owner of the newspaper, Davis Wright, was at the office now, called in by Ross. Nothing more had been found in the archive room other than some partial prints which would probably be useless given the filthy state of the place.

Zach drove as he talked, pulling up at the newspaper office as he ended the call with Ross. He went straight to the archive room to search again. He'd made a critical error last time he was down here, an assumption that had cost him precious time. He'd assumed that whoever took Grace had somehow gotten her out the front door without being noticed. It might have been possible if she'd been conscious, even under duress. Someone hauling an unconscious woman out the door would have attracted attention. If Lou Ann was telling the truth as he believed, no one had left by the front door. That meant there was another way out of that room.

Davis Wright was in a tailspin over the condition of his records room. Zach ignored his sputtering and began to search carefully, beginning at the sight where the struggle had occurred.

"I'm not sure what you're looking for, Sheriff."

"Another way out of this room." Zach straightened and faced Davis. "You know anything about that?"

Davis frowned. "Of course not. There's nothing down here but a closet. That's it."

"Where?"

"Over there," he pointed to the opposite end of the room. "Behind those stacked boxes."

Zach pushed and climbed his way across the mess, ignoring Davis' complaints about damage and destruction. He walked along the row to the end. Several of the stacks had been moved away from the wall and a small space appeared, just large enough for someone to squeeze through. Zach followed the tiny trail and came out amid a jumble of equipment littering the small floor space. Past that was the door to the closet.

Zach shoved an old vacuum out of the way with his foot and made his way to the door, Davis Wright following and cursing under his breath. Inside the closet was dark. Zach pulled the flashlight from his belt and passed it over the entire space of the closet. The six-by-eight-foot room held nothing but a string hanging down from the lone bulb on the ceiling. Zach pulled it and the room lit up. Nothing.

"I told you there was nothing here. I'm going back upstairs. You need to find out who's responsible for this mess, Sheriff. I mean it. Someone's going to pa—"

"You're not going anywhere, Davis. Stay put. We're not done here." Zach began to walk the perimeter of the room slowly, searching for signs of another door or a fake wall. On the far side of the closet he saw the crack in the wall running from floor to ceiling, and just big enough for him to get his fingers in. He handed the flashlight to Davis and used both hands to pull. The entire panel swung open and he stared into the darkness.

His heart pounded hard. His mind flipped ahead five years, ten, and he imagined what it would be like to never find Grace and to never know what had happened to her. That thought almost shut him down and he closed his eyes, forcing several deep breaths to get himself under control.

He remembered Andy's advice only hours earlier. *If you won't even pray for yourself...* He might not pray for himself, but he would do it for Grace.

Lord, I need your help. I'm not asking for myself. I know I don't deserve it. I'm asking for Grace. Please let her be all right. I need her to be okay. Please keep her safe wherever she is, and let her know somehow that I'm coming for her. And please help me find her soon.

Zach turned to Davis, one brow raised in question.

Davis raised his hand as if taking an oath in court. "I had no idea that was there, I swear."

The knot in Zach's gut tightened. He'd never had reason not to trust Davis. On the other hand, there were too many unanswered questions and things happening out of his control. He also had no desire to get trapped in a tunnel that led nowhere.

He made up his mind quickly. Grabbing Davis by the arm, he propelled him forward into the pitch-black tunnel. Davis immediately turned to come back out.

"I'm not going in there!"

"We're both going in there. I need to know where it leads, and I'm not leaving you here. And before you say anything else, let me remind you that your building was the scene of a kidnapping. You might want to consider cooperating."

He sputtered again, totally offended. "You can't possibly believe I had anything to do with that!"

Zach stared him down. "I'm not assuming anything at this point, and that includes your innocence. Let's go."

Davis stared at him, eyes wide with fear.

"Move!"

Davis reluctantly stepped into the tunnel lit by Zach's flashlight. As they moved through the narrow space Zach saw wooden bracings at intervals that reminded him of the mine shafts he saw in the westerns he loved. The floor was hard-packed dirt. Zach swung the light back and forth looking for signs of recent use. About ten yards in the dirt was softer and looked disturbed. Zach stopped Davis and crouched down to look, finding several large footprints, a man's boot. By the looks of it, the man carried extra weight on the left side. Was he carrying an unconscious Grace?

He stood and motioned Davis to keep moving. If his bearings were correct they would soon be close to the park in the center of town, heading for the other side of the town square. His mind raced ahead to the possibilities.

Davis kept looking back over his shoulder to see how far they'd come. Zach understood the feeling. The passageway behind them was now shrouded in blackness. It played tricks with his mind. He was ready to see sunlight again.

They continued walking for another twenty minutes, their pace slowed by the uneven ground and the need for caution. Suddenly they came to the end of the tunnel. No doorway was evident at first and Zach prayed they had not wasted the half hour on a literal dead end. He moved Davis out of the way and examined the walls closely. He missed it twice, but finally felt the small running crack that signaled a doorway. There was nothing to indicate the door, much less where it would lead. He pressed his ear to the door and tried to listen but heard nothing. He didn't trust the silence. Davis' eyes popped open wide as Zach drew his service revolver and motioned for him to open the door. Zach had his gun and flashlight pointed at the entrance, ready for whatever was behind it.

Davis pulled the door into the tunnel and light from the room spilled in, almost blinding them. Zach stepped in and knew immediately where they were. He lowered his weapon and clicked off his flashlight.

I should have known

Chapter Twenty-Six

Ross directed Forsythe's secretary to have a seat in the waiting room, far away from any files or computers that might be accessed and destroyed while they searched. The knuckles of her laced fingers were white, and her gaze shifted from one deputy to another.

"Where's your boss today?"

She shook her head. "I don't know. He left early yesterday and had me clear his calendar. I haven't heard from him since then. Sometimes he has meetings he doesn't tell me about."

Ross stared her down for a moment. Her eyes, filled with anxiety, never left his, not even to blink. If she knew anything she would have talked. She knew her boss well enough, though, to know there was plenty to be worried about.

Ross signaled to one of the deputies and pointed to the distraught woman sitting on the couch. "Watch her. She doesn't go near anything. No phone calls, and she doesn't leave until I say so."

"Yes, sir."

Two officers were already searching Forsythe's office. Ross wanted to make a quick sweep of the entire building so he headed down the hall to the conference room. As he approached he heard a strange scratching noise, then light footsteps. He drew his weapon, then stepped around the corner into the room.

He blew out a breath and holstered his weapon.

"Points for not shooting the boss." Zach shook his head, and pushed his fingers through his hair.

"Or your chief deputy," Ross agreed. "I guess this is where I ask where you came from?"

Zack glanced at Davis Wright still standing in the doorway to the tunnel, pale and wide-eyed.

"Davis," Ross acknowledged with a nod. "Ann's in the waiting room with a deputy. Why don't you join them?" Ross was polite enough, but the request stopped just short of being an order.

Now that he was out of the tunnel and still alive Davis looked irritated. "This has already taken too much of my time. I told you I didn't know anything and I need to get back to my office and start putting that mess back in order."

Zach stepped nose to nose with him. "I hope you're not involved in this, but like I said before, I can't assume anything right now, especially with a direct connection from your place to this one. We're going to figure it out, and you're going to stay here for now. If you're telling the truth you'll have my apology."

Davis' attempt at a stare-down was short, and he headed down the hall, muttering under his breath.

Ross waited until he was out of earshot, then looked at Zach, one brow cocked. "A secret tunnel?"

Zach nodded and took a seat at the conference table. "Yeah. If I hadn't seen it with my own eyes..."

"How'd you find it?"

"Davis told me there was a closet behind stacks of boxes. Someone had moved them out and the closet had been emptied. It didn't take long once we knew where to look."

"You think Davis is telling the truth?"

"Yeah. Probably not guilty of anything except not knowing what was going on in his own business. I'll let him sweat for a while then cut him loose. How's the search coming?"

"Just got started. We're starting with the files in his office."

Zach looked surprised. "How'd you get permission for that?"

"I told the judge we had a kidnapping, and I promised that

nothing we found in the files would be used against any of Forsythe's clients." He shrugged. "We wouldn't have the information anyway, so I figure we're not losing anything there, plus it's the only way we could search everything. It's going to take some time."

Zach pushed himself up from the table. "That's one thing we don't have. There's got to be a faster way to get this done."

"Yeah, someone could decide to talk to us but the people here don't seem to have a clue."

"Ann?"

Ross shook his head. "She knows enough to know that he's capable of some bad stuff, and she's scared, but nothing that will help us."

It was personal for Zach. That made it personal for Ross as well. The urgency he felt was matched by that of his boss, and Ross was at a loss to offer any comfort. He looked at his commander and friend. "We'll keep going until we find her."

Zach nodded. Ross knew they shared the same thought. Five people had been missing for more than forty years. If the same person had Grace, the manhunt they were starting could last the rest of their lives.

* * *

It's so cold in here. Why is it so cold in here?

Pulled awake by bone-deep chill, Grace reached down to pull up the covers – and woke in a flash of panic. She wasn't in bed and there were no covers. She couldn't do anything. Her hands and feet were bound and a thick rope around her waist held her even further. Her neck ached from the weight of her head hanging down as she slept or passed out. She wasn't sure which. Her jaw ached from clenching and she forced her mouth open to relax the muscles. Her extremities tingled with cold and lack of circulation and the shivering was becoming painful. She rocked herself – a tiny motion allowed by some give in the rope. It was hard to think. Her head pounded and the cold made her whole body ache. Her brain was a bit sluggish but she could still think.

C'mon, Grace! Get a grip.

She forced herself to slow her breathing. In through the nose. One, two, three, four, five. Out through the mouth. One, two, three, four, five, six, seven, eight, nine, ten. In through the nose…

She repeated the series, ruthlessly pushing out any thought but breathing. She lost count of the repetitions, but soon reaped the benefits of the exercise. The cold might eventually make it impossible to think clearly, but panic would render her helpless immediately.

She had to think. She wasn't dead so there must be a purpose for keeping her here. That meant that sooner or later someone would be coming here. Wherever here was.

She would negotiate. She was a counselor and knew how to talk to people, even very disturbed people. She sighed deeply. It was impossible to plan a strategy when she had no clue why she'd been brought here.

God, I don't know how long I can keep it together. I know you're here with me but I feel very alone. I don't know what's going to happen to me, but I can't stand waiting. I feel like I'm going insane. Please take care of me. I don't wan-

Creeeak.

Chapter Twenty-Seven

"Sheriff, think you'll want to see this."

Zach took the proffered file from his deputy and opened it on the table. It was a will. Grace Tucker's will. He spun the file around and pointed Ross to it. He heard Ross' sharp intake of breath and nodded.

Ross shook his head. "I don't believe it."

"Neither do I. Grace despises Forsythe. She would never come to him for legal advice." He shook his head. "She met with that guy from her hometown, the attorney. What was his name?"

Ross thought a moment. "Mark something."

"Yeah, well whoever. It wouldn't have been Forsythe." Zach sat back and began to read through the will. It was short and to the point. And as suspicious as a convenience store customer in a ski mask. Zach snorted in disgust.

"What?"

"How did he think he was going to get away with this?" He shook his head and held up the file. "According to this she made two bequests. The executor of her estate gets five hundred-thousand dollars. Any guess as to who that might be?"

"Remington Forsythe, I presume?"

"Very astute."

Ross shrugged. "I've been told I'm a fairly decent investigator."

"All right, then, want to take a stab at who gets the rest of the estate?"

Ross thought for a moment. "I give up."

Zach watched Ross closely as he answered. "Martin Tucker."

Ross' brow shot up. "The Martin Tucker that disappeared forty years ago? That Martin Tucker?"

"Junior." Zach slapped the file closed. "According to this, Tuck's brother had one son."

Ross leaned back in his chair. "Right. So, someone neither of us has ever heard of ends up in the will of a woman who couldn't possibly know him. Sound right to you?"

Zach slapped the file closed. "I think Forsythe has gone off the chain this time." He got up and paced to the window. "For anyone to inherit, Grace has to die." He'd been thinking about it all day since finding the chloroformed rag in the archives room. A part of him denied it, kept thinking whoever took Grace meant to hold her for ransom. The discovery of this will chilled him to the core.

Ross stood as well. "I'll get Renee on it. Maybe she can track down Martin, Jr., or at least give us somewhere to start."

Zach just nodded. "It's already signed, Ross."

"What?"

"The will. It's already signed. Forged." He looked back at Ross. "Which means he doesn't need her anymore. She may already be dead."

* * *

"Who's there?"

Grace strained to hear something. Anything. Her heart beat so loudly in her ears it drowned out every other sound.

"I know you're there. Say something!"

The rasping crackling of a match strike shot another jolt of adrenaline through her. The brief flare of the tiny flame forced her eyes closed. She twisted as far as she could to see behind her until the pain from her shackles forced her to quit. Smoke curled around her head – cigar smoke. Someone stood directly behind her, his breath close enough to ruffle her hair. She ducked her head searching for a breath of

179

clean air but found none. She coughed and tears ran from her burning eyes.

"Wh-what do you want?"

Say something!

Silence screamed through her. She was going to die. She braced for the pain of a knife or bullet. Maybe he would just wrap his hands around her throat and squeeze until she—

"Hello, Grace."

She jerked in her chair and pain coursed through her. Footsteps circled around to the front. The glowing end of the cigar cast an eerie light on a face, both exposing and concealing it in shadows.

Grace leaned forward as much as she could. "Who are you? Why did you bring me here?"

"All in good time. I just came to have a look at you." He made a tsking sound. "All this trouble you've caused. I can't imagine why Tobias even bothered."

"Where am I?"

He laughed and chills crawled all over her. "You're in the secret place, Grace. Tobias's secret place. You wanted to know the family secret, didn't you? Well, you're sitting in it."

"I don't understand. What—"

"Everything you don't want to know about is down here. You think you'll feel better once you know everything but you won't."

She believed him. "Please. It's so cold in here. Please let me go."

"No."

He turned abruptly and walked away from her.

"Wait! Don't leave me here!"

He stopped. "I'll be back. And then you'll wish I'd stayed away."

* * *

Dani woke with a bad feeling. Light from the muted TV screen flickered in strange patterns, and she reached for the remote to turn it off. She pushed herself into a sitting position and sat in the dark trying to remember her dream and why it fueled such a sense of dread.

Grace.

She sounded fine when I talked to her.

Dani reached for her cell and started to call, then noticed the time. One thirty-five. She put her phone down.

What are you gonna do, wake her up and say, 'Sorry, I had a bad dream about you, just wanted to be sure you were sleeping okay'?

She settled back into the deep couch cushions and pulled an afghan around her shoulders to combat the slight chill. After several minutes her body warmed but her soul still shook.

Something's wrong.

She reached for her phone again and this time didn't hesitate to complete the call. If she woke Grace and everything was fine, well, Grace would understand, they'd have a good laugh and then get some sleep.

The call went straight to voice mail. Grace always answered her phone unless she was with a patient. It was the middle of the night. Where else would she be besides in bed? Maybe she was just sleeping hard and didn't hear the phone. Maybe.

Maybe she's in the bathroom. I'll give her a minute and call again.

She did. Several times in a row, not concerned anymore with waking her up. Now she was worried about Grace not being able to answer. That was so much worse.

Every unanswered call shredded her nerves. The next time she got Grace's voice mail she left a message. Short and to the point.

"Grace, it's Dani. I'm on the way to you."

* * *

Zach picked up the paper cup of coffee then put it down without drinking. It was hours old and cold. Even hot it had been some of the worst he'd ever tasted. He looked across the office to where Ross sat going through files. He had the look of a man exhausted but determined to complete a mission. He needed sleep. They both did.

Zach glanced at his watch. Two-fifteen. He pressed the heels of his hands into his eyes and rubbed. This was getting them nowhere. Forsythe's files – while a disturbing record of dysfunction and depravity – held no clue to where Grace might be or where they might find Martin Tucker, Jr. He was sick of reading them. Sometimes it was better not to know things – especially when you couldn't do anything about them. After reading these files he was going to have trouble looking some people in the eye ever again. The small-town gossip that raced along the grapevine was just the tip of the iceberg. Zach had never been naive, but the things he'd read in the last few hours left him heartsick.

"You got anything?"

Zach lifted his head wearily. "More than I ever wanted to know. And nothing I need." He pushed back from the desk and walked to the window, peering out at the sleeping town. His town. His home. It hadn't felt like that since Henry died. Now he wondered if it could ever feel like home again.

The chair creaked as Ross stood and joined Zach at the window. "Looks peaceful, doesn't it?" He pushed his hands in his pockets and leaned his shoulder against the wall to face Zach. "You'd never know there was so much blackmail material out there."

"You think that's what he's doing?"

Ross shrugged. "He blackmailed Lou Ann, didn't he? We know he's not above it. It would certainly explain his lifestyle. I know lawyers make good money, but this is a small town with small town cases. I never really saw how he was making that much money. He was always driving new, expensive cars, always eating out, having work done on his house. Flashy clothes and jewelry. It's got to be coming from somewhere."

Zach looked at the man he trusted more than anyone on earth after Henry. Maybe Henry should never have been at the top of that list. It had to be said, and there was no one alive he could say it to but Ross.

"I'm afraid of what we're going to find out if we keep looking."

Ross said nothing, just waited patiently.

Zach continued because after everything, he needed to know that he could at least be honest with himself.

"I think we're going to find a file on Henry somewhere in all this mess and I think it's going to be bad. I think before this is over I won't even know my own grandfather." He glanced up at his friend. "Now would be a great time for you to tell me I'm way off base and just sleep deprived."

Ross stayed silent for a long time. "It won't change the good things, Zach," he said quietly. "Can you remember that while we're looking? Henry wasn't perfect. You may be right. You may be about to find out things that you should never have to know about him, but you need to remember the good. I'm not excusing whatever he did – and it may be as bad as you think – but try to keep an open mind. Henry was strong, but sometimes people – even strong people – get caught up in things beyond their control and make bad decisions in the moment that follow them for the rest of their lives. Whatever we find we'll deal with. If there's a way to make it right, we will. If not," he shrugged, "you'll find a way to live with it, and eventually forgive him."

Zach pushed away from the window and paced down the length of the conference table stopping at the place he'd been planted for hours reading files. He rubbed his eyes, the grit in them vied with the acid in his stomach to see which would cause him the most discomfort. Exhaustion that should have put him down instead made him antsy. Retaliation for being ignored.

"Well, look at this."

Zach turned to see Ross crouched down in front on a small cabinet. He assumed it was a personal refrigerator.

"Got anything with caffeine in there?"

"Better."

"What could be better?"

"A safe."

Zach headed over and leaned over Ross' shoulder to see. "Can you open it?"

Ross grabbed the handle and gave it a yank.

"I guess that would be too easy," Zach said, when it didn't budge.

They looked at one another for a long moment.

"I can have a tech with a drill here in twenty minutes," Ross offered.

Zach nodded. "Do it. While we wait, I'm going for coffee." He hesitated for a moment. "Not sure if a safe is included in the warrant." He drummed his fingers on the table. "Go ahead. If it's not included then we'll go with your personal motto."

Ross grinned. "Easier to ask forgiveness than permission."

* * *

Exhaustion and cold once again pulled Grace from sleep. After countless cycles, she'd lost track of how many times she'd dozed off and even more frightening, how long she'd been in this dark hole.

They won't have to kill you. They'll just leave you here to die. In the dark. Just like you did, Tobias. You left me in the dark and now look what's happened. You're no different than they are.

"I wish I'd never heard from you!" She yelled it into the darkness and heard the echo in the cavernous space. Anger replaced despair and it felt good. It felt strong. She might go down, but she would never give up. Never! She began to move the little bit she could, contracting muscles, trying to warm them up. She tried to think of what she could say the next time someone came. If she got him talking long enough she might be able to convince him to loosen the rope and chains holding her to the chair. Anything would help.

She was hungry and thirsty, and she needed to go to the bathroom. The need was rather urgent now and the cold made it worse.

Don't think about it, Grace. Yeah, that's helpful.

She gave another yank on the ropes.

"You'll hurt yourself if you keep that up."

Grace jumped and let out a squeal of surprise. "Who's there?" She hadn't heard anyone come in. How long had they been there watching and listening? "Please tell me why you've brought me here."

A single yellow bulb flashed overhead. Grace squinted and ducked her head against the pain of sudden illumination. For a moment she was as blind as she'd been in the total darkness. She cautiously cracked one eye open, then the other. The light was dim and cast an eerie yellow glow around the room, but it was enough.

Remington Forsythe stood in front of her, aiming her own gun right at her head.

Chapter Twenty-Eight

"Hello, Grace." He tilted his head to one side as he studied her. "You don't seem surprised to see me."

Adrenaline shot through her system flooding her with heat. "I should have known. Why did you bring me here?"

While she waited for his answer she took her first look at the place that had been her prison. The room was fairly big. Hallways branched off three sides, dark and uninviting. There were no windows and she didn't see a door. They were totally isolated. It was the perfect place for…whatever this was.

Forsythe pulled up a chair and sat down facing her. He crossed his legs casually and rested the arm holding her gun across his lap. "People who know too much can be dangerous."

"I don't know *anything!*"

"Ah, yes, well I know that now, but I couldn't take a chance, could I? I had to act – preemptive strike as it were – to protect my interests. It would seem I acted in haste, but that," he waved a hand back and forth in the air, "is all water under the bridge now. What's done is done, eh?"

"*You* are so done!"

Anger clouded his face and he leaned forward, so close she could smell his rancid breath. "I am not the one tied up and tucked away for safe keeping. I am not the one who will live out the rest of my days in this hole. You would do well, Ms. Tucker, to keep in mind who is in charge here."

"Untie me."

Forsythe snorted with laughter. "I don't think so, Grace. You might as well get comfortable. You're going to be here for…ever."

"I need to go to the bathroom. Let me up."

"That's too bad," he snapped. "You're not getting out of that chair."

Grace forced herself to sit back and relax as much as possible. He would feed on her fear and desperation. "You're afraid of me, aren't you," she taunted. "Even holding a gun on me you're afraid."

He snorted again. "Don't be ridiculous. You don't scare me."

"Then prove it. Let me go to the bathroom. Or would it be too easy for me to get away from you and get out of here?"

He stared at her. She glared right back, daring him to do it. He blinked and she felt a surge of hope. He walked to her and reached down to release her ankles. She couldn't suppress a tiny groan as she forced her legs to stretch out in front of her. He stepped behind her and released the rope that held her to the chair. All that was left was rope securing her hands behind her back. He worked on the knot until it loosened, then he stopped. Grace held her breath, willing him to continue.

Cold steel pressed against her temple so hard her head tilted to the side.

"Don't you move until I say so. If you try anything I'll blow your brains out."

She didn't bother to tell him that after hours of sitting immobile in the cold she was not capable of moving fast or with much coordination. She simply nodded her head, acknowledging the threat.

The rope fell away and her arms dropped to her sides. She spent a long moment just breathing deeply and relishing her freedom. She crossed her arms over her chest and hugged herself trying to warm up, then rubbed her palms up and down her thighs. The friction created just a bit of heat but it felt like heaven.

"Let's go."

Forsythe watched her with his little weasel eyes. This was the man who had dared to enter her home. Who had planned to steal from her and then when he got caught, had the audacity to whine to the sheriff about hi—

Zach. Zach will be looking for me.

Hope flared for a moment. She had missed an appointment at the bank with Ross. He would want to know why. All she had to do was stay alive. They would find her. Grace pushed herself up and clung to the back of the chair to steady herself. She moved like an old woman as she stepped around the chair and straightened. She cocked a brow at Forsythe, waiting for directions.

He waved the gun to his left and squinted, trying to see. He flipped a switch and a small section of the corridor lit up. She started that way slowly. They moved down the hall together, Grace trailing her hand along the wall for support. The weakness scared her. Cold, fear, lack of food and water for hours. The combination had taken a toll on her.

They came to a bend in the hallway and Forsythe stopped her. "Right here," he said. "I'll be waiting. Make it fast or I'll come in and get you. Don't get any ideas." He sounded mean, but he looked less worried than before. She had looked weak walking down the hall.

Grace entered the tiny room and flicked on the light. She enjoyed slamming the door in Forsythe's face. No lock, but it didn't matter. While she took care of business, she scanned the room for anything she could use as a weapon. Not much, but she managed to find one or two things that might work if her timing was good and luck was on her side.

Forsythe banged on the door making her jump.

"Hurry up."

"I'm coming. Just one more minute." She took her time washing her hands while she went over her plan. She would get one shot. If it didn't work, she could very well end up dead. She took a deep breath and opened the door.

* * *

Ross thanked the tech he'd roused out of bed and sent him home again. He knelt by the safe and swung the door all the way open. It was divided into two sections. The space on the bottom was completely filled with cash. Ross ignored that and reached for the stack of envelopes in the top section. He carried them to the table and shoved everything else away to make room. He tore into the first envelope and slid the contents out onto the table. Papers, smaller envelopes, and a tiny cassette. Ross picked it up with gloved hands and looked at the writing on the label. It was written in permanent ink, faded and yellowed with age. The single word made Ross's gut clench: Tucker.

Ross turned the tape over and over in his hand, not liking where this was going. Whatever was on this tape would change what he knew about this town's history, what he knew about Tuck. If there was a tape for Tobias, there was probably one for Henry. He opened the second envelope. More papers and another cassette. He knew before he looked at the label what it would say. He flipped it over, then closed his eyes and blew out a long breath. He hated to be right. He looked around for something to play the tapes on. If he could listen to them before Zach got back maybe he could spare his friend – at least for a little while.

"Play them."

The quiet voice startled Ross and he looked up to see Zach standing in the doorway watching him.

"Zach, why don't we—"

"Play them, Ross. Let's just get it over with."

Ross studied his friend closely, then nodded and rose to rifle through the desk to find a machine that would play the tapes. He found one in a drawer under a pile of junk and brought it to the table. The tape labeled Tucker had the earliest date so he started with that one. He clicked play, turned up the volume and braced himself for what they were about to hear.

* * *

Grace opened the door slowly and made a show of drying her hands. She crumpled the paper towel in her hand and reached back in the bathroom to throw it away. She dropped the towel and grabbed the can of air freshener. As she backed out of the bathroom she whipped around and brought the can up, spraying the stuff directly into Forsythe's eyes. He screamed and brought his free hand to his face rubbing frantically to clear his vision. Grace dropped the can and reached back for the tank lid she had placed carefully by the door. She brought it up with both hands and swung at his head as he fired blindly. She hit low and his shoulder took the brunt of the first swing. It was heavy enough that it swung her around forcing her to swing backhanded the second time. A sickening crack silenced his screams abruptly and he dropped to the floor like wet cement. She dropped the lid, which shattered loudly on the floor. A moment later, screaming pain registered in her left arm and she looked to see blood dripping down her arm.

The quiet was so intense she heard every drop of blood hit the floor. She leaned back against the door to steady herself as she looked at Forsythe's still form. Too still. Head wounds bled profusely, but even so, there was an alarmingly large pool of blood beneath his head. The crack sounded again and again in her head as she forced herself to check for a pulse. Nothing.

Forsythe was dead.

She had killed him.

Her stomach lurched and she stumbled back inside the bathroom just in time to be sick. Everything in her was screaming for her to run. Forsythe was dead, but there was another one. Someone who could return at any minute. She didn't have much fight left, maybe enough to get out of here and get help, but she had to move.

She rinsed her mouth out, then ripped off her sleeve and used it as a bandage for her arm. The bullet hadn't penetrated her arm, just made a deep crease on the side. A flesh wound. Only a flesh wound. Only someone who'd never had one would say that. She tied the bandage as tight as she could manage one-handed and washed the blood off as best she could. It was under her nails but she didn't have time to worry about that. She splashed cold water on her face. It helped a little but she was still not prepared for the gaunt, haunted looking woman who stared back at her from the mirror. She had taken a life.

You had no choice. He was going to leave you here to die. Get over it and get out of here.

Grace prayed for strength and wisdom. It's not like she had a lot of experience escaping crazed killers. She made herself lean over Forsythe to retrieve the gun and the flashlight. The quiet was deafening as she made her way down the hall back to the room where she had been imprisoned. Like a tomb. Chills broke out all over her body that had nothing to do with the temperature. She still had no idea where she was, but she felt certain that no one would just happen to find her.

She stepped into the yellow light of the large room and looked for an exit. Forsythe had gotten in somehow. And so had someone else. Someone who had promised to come back. There was no way out of this room except down one of the hallways. No cracks indicating a hidden door. No stairs. Nothing. Grace forced herself to move back down the corridor. She gave Forsythe's body a wide berth, half expecting him to jump up and tackle her as she went by. The corridor stretched far beyond the reach of her flashlight and she saw no other switches indicating lights. When she turned to look behind her all she saw was darkness. It surrounded her outside the small bubble of light from the flashlight. Disorienting. She moved slowly, examining the walls as she went, and stopping to listen for sounds of the other man returning.

After she stumbled a third time she stopped walking and slid down the wall to sit and rest. She tried not to think about how hard it would be to get up. Cold continued to leach strength from her. The wound in her arm burned like crazy but the pain kept her grounded, and she was grateful. After allowing herself a short rest she pushed to her feet, determined not to stop again until she was out of this place or dropped from sheer exhaustion.

Jesus, please keep me going. I can't do it by myself.

She kept moving, body and brain numb. She stumbled again and went down hard, banging her knees on the unforgiving floor and sending the gun and the flashlight skidding away from her. She pushed up on her good arm and lifted her head. Nothing. She was done. She swept her good arm out feeling for the gun. She bumped the flashlight and it rolled away from her. The beam of light passed over something. She reached for it again, raised the light and swung it back and forth. A small sob escaped as she crawled her way to steps built into the wall. They went on forever, past the beam of light, but she didn't care. She kept crawling up those stairs to the top, and the door that led the way out of here. It had to. Hope gave her strength and she grasped to door handle, half expecting it to be locked. It turned easily and she pushed out with the last bit of energy she had. The door swung open and she lurched out into the early morning, sucking in deep breaths of fresh air.

She turned slowly, trying to figure out where she was. She was standing on a concrete platform with a doorway above ground. She shivered. It looked like the bunker she had seen with Zach, only different than what she remembered. She faced away from the small building to take in the area around her. The sun peeked over the clouds in the distance, shooting out fingers of pink and orange and yellow. It was the most beautiful sight she'd ever seen. She headed for the steps that would take her to ground level. The highway in the distance looked to be about a half a mile away. If she could stay on her feet she could be there in about ten minutes. Maybe fifteen. She could flag down a car and get back to civilization. It was almost over.

"Hello, Grace. I told you I'd come back."

Chapter Twenty-Nine

Zach stared out the window of Forsythe's office watching the first rays of sunlight peek over the horizon and listening to Henry's voice on tape explaining why they would keep the whereabouts of the five missing men a secret. It was the only way they could keep the details of the crime – specifically who was responsible – a secret. Henry would do this for, Tobias, his lifelong friend. A friend who had now committed his own horrendous crime. The crime had brought an end to the disappearances, but would forever haunt this county, and if known, would bring shame on his family for generations to come. There was no fixing what had happened. The men were dead. The families wouldn't get closure, but there was no help for it. That happened all the time. They would learn to live with it.

Ross stopped the tape. Zach rested his forehead against the window. He was the world's biggest fraud. Generations of his family had served and protected this town – until Henry. It wasn't enough that he was dead. Now the memory of him was lost forever. It shouldn't have been such a big loss; after all it had all been a lie.

What am I supposed to do with this, Henry? Did you really think no one would find out? How am I supposed to face this town knowing what you did?

A hand clapped down on his shoulder. "It doesn't change the good things." Ross's quiet statement pulled his attention back inside. "Try to remember that."

Zach felt lacerated. He was bleeding from a thousand invisible wounds. "What was he thinking? How do you go from being the sheriff to being an accomplice to murder? Five murders." He pushed away from the window to pace. "It's like a bad movie. The good ol' boys just taking care of each other, no matter what. He *knew*, Ross. All these years he knew what happened to those men and he just let those families suffer. What kind of sheriff does that? What kind of *man* does that? And Grace. What is she supposed to think? Her grandfather killed his own brother."

"To stop the other killings, yes." Ross held up a hand to stop Zach's response. "It was wrong. In every sense, on every level, it was wrong. Zach, think about how you feel knowing what Henry did. He didn't kill anyone, but you still feel ashamed of what he did. Imagine how Tobias felt when he found out his only brother was killing people in their own town. Their friends."

"My whole life with him was a lie. All those times we spent together – I thought he was the greatest man alive. The whole time he knew and he never said anything. I don't even know who he was anymore." Zach whirled around and smashed his fist into the wall. Pain radiated all the way to his shoulder and for one brief moment eclipsed the agony in his heart.

"Feel better?"

Zach glared at Ross. "Don't start with me, Ross. You have no idea—"

"No, I don't," Ross said quietly. "Here's the thing. Henry and Tuck made some colossally bad decisions before you were born. You're not responsible for that. Never were. You're the sheriff *now*. You have a kidnapping to deal with and five unsolved murders to address. You're responsible for what you do with those things now. The way I see it, you're in the same boat as Grace. She's not responsible for what Tuck did, and she sure can't bring those people back, but the two of you can put it to rest once and for all, and give those families closure. Someone was afraid she was going to do just that, and that's why they took her."

"Forsythe." Zach spit the name through clenched teeth.

"Maybe," Ross answered. "I don't think he was in this alone. As an attorney, he couldn't be held accountable for any crime his client had already committed, only one he had prior knowledge of, right?"

Ross was trying to pull him back into law enforcement mode. "Yeah. Right." Zach forced his brain to process what they'd read through the last eighteen hours.

"So who else stood to lose if all of this came out in the open?"

"Tuck. But he was going to tell Grace everything. Henry."

"Was also killed. I don't think this was about protecting Henry. Who else?"

"Martin Tucker, Jr."

"Exactly. No one even knew he existed. At least I've never heard anyone speak of him, but apparently he's been alive and well and waiting for a chance to cash in."

"And he needed Forsythe to help him." Zach paced the room again, this time with energy generated from forward progress on the case. Finally.

"He set Grace up, and now he's got her somewhere. For what?" Zach stopped at the table again, tapping his knuckles as he thought through everything. "He's already forged her signature so he doesn't need her anymore. What's to stop him from killing her?" He stopped and locked eyes with Ross. "Or just making her disappear like those men." He pushed down his fear for Grace. He couldn't be distracted by it. "Those men are somewhere in this county. I'd bet my life on it. We find them, we find Grace."

Ross gathered up the files and stacked them on the end of the table. "I'm going to call Alan and have him meet me at the title office. It's Saturday, so I'll probably have to bribe him with breakfast, but he'll do it. I should have a list of all the properties owned by Forsythe, Henry, and Tuck in an hour. We'll check every one of them. This is something you'd want to keep close to home, so maybe we'll get lucky."

Zach nodded. "Keep me posted. I'm going to Grace's. She

found those newspaper clippings in the attic. I'm going to see if I can find anything else." He headed for the door but turned back for a second. "Ross, thanks."

Ross nodded. "We'll find her. And we'll make this right."

Zach nodded once, and set off to do just that.

Chapter Thirty

In her haste to get up the stairs and out of the bunker Grace had not taken the time to find and retrieve the gun after she fell. That mistake could now cost her life. Her brain screamed at her to run, but her body could not obey. Exhausted, terrified, and completely spent, she dropped to her knees.

The man who towered over her looked familiar. She tried to focus but tears of frustration and fear distorted his image.

"Who are you?" she whispered.

A sick grin split his face as he leaned down close to her. "I'm your cousin, Grace. Cousin Martin at your service." He bowed and swept his hand toward her. "To be precise, Tobias Tucker and my father were brothers. You father was my first cousin. That makes us second cousins. Nice to finally make your acquaintance."

Grace licked her dry, cracked lips and tried to focus. She turned her head toward the highway and felt hope slip away. What had seemed manageable only moments ago was now impossible. She was not sure she could even stand on her own let alone walk a half mile to the road. She looked back at Martin. He would never let her get there anyway and she couldn't fight him. She sank back against the wall, heartsick and furious with herself for leaving the gun behind when she wasn't safe yet.

Martin grinned at her. "That's better. I was hoping you wouldn't be stupid enough to try to get away. You can't, you know. It would mess up everything and I can't allow that." He hunkered down in front of her. "I saw what you did to Forsythe. Saves me from having to kill him myself, the idiot." He grabbed her chin hard and yanked it up so she had to look him straight in the eyes. "You won't get a chance to kill me so don't even think about it, *Cousin Grace.* I want to show you something, but if you give me too much trouble I'll just go ahead and kill you now, got it?"

She tried to speak but the energy was just not there anymore. She nodded and closed her eyes.

"Good. Now when you wake up we'll be in my special place. Our family's special place, and you'll finally know the secret. Then it will be your special place, too. And you'll never want to leave."

When you wake up…

The words registered as she felt the sting of a needle in her neck and then the world went black.

* * *

"She's not here." Lucy pounded on the front door again.

Dani came around the corner. "Her car's gone." She stood on the porch, hands on hips, and slowly scanned the property from one side to the other. "Where would she be at this time of the morning?"

Lucy shook her head, her sense of unease growing. "That's just it. She doesn't really know anyone in town; nothing's open. Besides, when have you ever known her to miss a chance to sleep late?"

"She hasn't answered her phone for over twenty-four hours," Dani said quietly.

"Yeah, there's that, too." Lucy huffed out a breath. It was not in her nature to wait, and unanswered questions – especially this unanswered question – made her crazy. "Well, I'm not gonna just stand around out here. I'm going in."

Dani spun to face her, surprised. "You mean you're breaking in."

"Whatever. You can stand out here if you want to but we both know something's wrong. Maybe something inside will tell us what's going on. If not, we'll call that sheriff."

"Yeah, okay, just hurry. I'm so worried."

Lucy reached over and plucked two bobby pins from Dani's messy bun and had the lock picked in less than a minute. She opened the door and turned back to grin at Dani. "Don't ask me where I learned to do that."

Dani stared in outright admiration. "I won't, but can you teach me?"

Lucy handed back the bobby pins. "When we find Grace I'll teach both of you." She pushed the door open and stepped inside, Dani on her heels.

They moved through the first floor together checking every room. "It's neat as a pin," Dani said quietly.

Lucy nodded solemnly. "Yeah, if something happened, it wasn't here."

Lucy made her way to the kitchen. No dishes in the sink. No food on the stove. No sign the Grace had been interrupted in the middle of anything. It was perfect. And so wrong. She went to Grace's room and found the bed neatly made, clothes put away.

Where are you, Grace?"

She met Dani coming down the hall and shook her head. "Nothing."

"Me either. I don't want to overreact. Nothing here looks out of place. Maybe…"

"I don't think we're overreacting, and I think it's time to call the sheriff."

"Okay, but first I want to run up to the attic, just to look around. I'll be right back."

Lucy went back to the kitchen. She pulled open the refrigerator door and stood there staring inside, then huffed out her frustration. She wasn't going to find anything in there. She slammed the door and turned to leave then stopped as she caught sight of a box on the counter. It was small and flat and looked like it had been around for about a hundred years. She sat down at the island to explore while she waited for Dani. Inside she found a stack of newspaper clippings, yellowed and brittle. And she read. Her stomach knotted tighter as she read through the stories. What in the world had Grace gotten herself into?

"Lucy! Get up here!"

She hit the ground at a dead run.

* * *

Zach headed to Grace's house with lights flashing, thankful there wasn't much traffic this early. He tried to think like a cop, focus on facts and see where they led him. Forsythe was in this up to his little weasel eyes. Martin Tucker, too. Where had he been all these years, and more to the point, where was he now?

Zach's cell rang and Ross's name appeared in the screen. "Ross, any news on Martin Tucker?"

"That's why I'm calling. Renee's done excellent work as usual. She found him, alive and well and hiding in plain sight, just across the state line."

Zach drew in a deep breath. *Finally!* "What do we know?"

"He applied for and got disability when he was twenty-four for, and I quote, 'a mental or nervous disorder that impaired his ability to maintain gainful employment', if you can believe that."

"The mental disorder part I have no trouble believing. What else?"

"He's been living in Brentwood with his mother. Moved there about a month after his dad went missing. She died five years ago and he inherited the house. Neighbors say he keeps to himself for the most part. Goes out of town for long weekends sometimes. No one knows where he goes or what he does. They think he's a little odd, so they avoid him.

They don't bother him, he doesn't bother them."

"Where is he now?"

"Unknown. He's been gone longer than usual this time, almost a full week. I checked with the local cops. No one's at the house but nothing looks unusual. Mail and papers have been stopped indefinitely. He's just gone."

Zach processed for a moment. "We need to get inside."

"Do we have enough for a warrant?"

"We have a kidnapping. He could be holding a woman against her will. That should at least get them in under the pretense of a welfare check." Zach was silent for a moment. "Call them back, Ross. Tell them what's going on here. See if they'll go in and check out the house. It's probably a dead end but I want to look at every possibility."

"I'll get on it. Where are you now?"

"Almost to Grace's house. I'm going back to check on—"

"Zach? What is it?"

"Car there I don't recognize. Run this plate." Zach read off the tag number fast. "I'm going to check it out. I'll call you in a minute."

"I'm headed there now. Wait for me."

"Can't wait. We can't afford to miss anything." He clicked off the phone, shutting down some very colorful language from his second-in-command. He turned down a dirt road that took him close to the side of the house. Trees and untamed bushes provided cover as he left his car with his binoculars. He found a spot between two small trees and crouched down as he began to scan the house, starting with the downstairs windows. His pulse raced and he forced himself to breath slow and deep. He saw nothing on the first floor and quickly moved to the second. Nothing. He raised the binoculars to the attic window then dropped his arms as he tried to decide whether to laugh or swear.

He jogged back to his car and called Ross.

"You're never gonna believe who owns that car," Ross said.

"Dani or the little spitfire. Grace's friends."

"How did you—"

"I saw them through the window. They're in the attic. I don't know what they're up to but I'm about to find out. I'll call you when I know something."

"Look behind you."

Zach turned just as Ross passed the dirt road and turned into the driveway. He followed him and they met up on the porch.

Zach rolled his eyes. "You don't think they're dangerous, do you?"

Ross snorted. "Of course not. I just don't want to miss any part of this. It oughta be good."

Zach tried the knob and it turned easily. He stepped inside quietly, Ross right behind him, both had hands on weapons. They moved carefully from room to room and found nothing. The quiet sounds of someone moving around in the attic confirmed what he'd seen through the window, but protocol was protocol. You don't move on until the area is clear. They moved quickly now, making their way to the next floor. Nothing out of place. Ross pointed to the attic and Zach nodded.

The door to the attic stairs was open, not typical when Tuck had lived here. A lot of things weren't like when Tuck was alive anymore. Zach pushed down a fresh wave of grief and continued up the stairs. As he approached he heard the women speaking. He couldn't make out the words but the tone was clear. They were scared.

Zach took another step and the floor creaked beneath his weight. Immediately the voices stopped, replaced by deafening silence. Tension flowed from that room in thick waves. Zach looked at Ross who nodded. Weapon in hand, Zach took one more step.

"Ladies, this is Sheriff Wells. I'm with a deputy. We're coming in. Is everyone all right?"

A long pause. "We're fine, Sheriff. Come on in."

They stepped into the attic where the two women waited with

guns aimed at the door and a take-no-prisoners look on their faces.

Time stopped as all four faced one another, not moving. Barely breathing.

Zach took a breath and held up his free hand while he holstered his weapon. "Just us, ladies. Why don't we start with everyone putting down their guns?"

Both women looked at Ross who managed a tight smile. "Ladies first."

"Something's happened to Grace."

Zach nodded. "We know. I'll fill you in, but guns down first."

He watched in amazement as both guns disappeared into what had to be clothing specially designed to conceal weapons. He glanced at Ross who rolled his eyes and holstered his own weapon.

"Why don't you tell us how you know something's wrong?"

"Why don't you just tell us what happened?"

That was the little spitfire. *What is her name?*

"Lucy, just tell him so we can figure out how to help Grace."

Lucy. That's it.

She looked him straight in the eye. "We've been trying to get in touch with her since early yesterday. Dani's been leaving messages and texting. It's not like Grace to not answer unless she's with a patient, which clearly, she's not. She hasn't exactly gotten a warm welcome in this town, and in case you've forgotten, that attorney broke in here once already. I don't think it was unreasonable to assume that something's wrong." She stopped and drew a deep shaky breath. "And then we came here and found these."

Dani lifted a small metal box from the little table behind her.

Zach took it from her trembling, outstretched hand, and slowly opened the lid. A small envelope nestled in the box and he lifted it out and slid the contents into his hand. Five Polaroid pictures, each one of a man sitting in a chair. More accurately, *tied* to a chair.

And dead.

Very, very dead.

Chapter Thirty-One

"Good, you're awake. I was getting bored watching you sleep."

Adrenaline shot Grace fully awake. That voice. She tried to push herself up from the floor but one arm was chained to the wall and the other collapsed under her. She groaned and rested her head on the cold concrete, fighting nausea and fear. Panic would get her killed. She needed to think.

She closed her eyes and dragged in lungs full of the chilled air. After several moments her rebellious stomach stopped kicking so hard. Grace forced her clenched jaws to relax but didn't move, even to take a look at her captor.

Just breathe. In. Out. You will not get sick! Just breathe.

"Sorry about drugging you again. I needed to get you back inside without a fight."

Grace didn't bother to open her eyes. "Why did you bring me here? What do you want?"

"Oh no, it's what *you* want, Cousin Grace. You wanted to know the secret. I'm going to tell you. Actually, I'm going to show it to you. Aren't you going to ask where we are?"

Grace pushed herself up and leaned against the wall. Her jaws clenched again. It was so cold. She tipped her head back and looked at the man who held her prisoner. Her cousin. Family. The family she'd been so eager to know.

Be careful what you wish for, Grace. Too late now.

"F-fine. Where are w-we?"

205

"Oh, you're cold, aren't you? I'm sorry about that but heat would be bad in here."

Grace frowned. He wasn't making sense. Maybe she was the one not making sense. He was right there in front of her, grinning like an idiot, but he sounded so far away.

He dragged a metal chair across the concrete, the sound like nails on a chalkboard, and sat down right in front of her. He opened a thermos and her attention laser focused on the steam rising from the coffee. Without thought she leaned close, seeking heat.

He poured a cup and raised it to his lips, then looked at her sadly. "I'm sorry, cousin, but there's only enough for one. I'd share, but I need to stay sharp so I can tell you a story."

He took a sip, sighed, and smirked.

Grace leaned back against the wall and let her eyes close. It was too much. She'd been free and now…surely someone was looking for her now. It had been – how long? Hours? Days? She didn't care anymore. She just wanted to go to sleep and get away from the cold and her insane cousin. She didn't want to know the family secret anymore, but she was very afraid it was about to be buried all over again, and her right along with it.

"I'm n-not interest-sted."

"But of course you are, Grace. It's what you came here for. It's why Uncle Tobias sent for you. It's the story of our family, and you get to be a part of it now, take your rightful place."

She refused to engage with him anymore. It wouldn't matter. Whatever was going to happen, she couldn't stop it.

He took another sip of coffee and pulled a candy bar from his pocket. "I'm afraid I can't share this either. Are you very hungry? Let me take your mind off that. Listen up. Once upon a time there was a young man who did a very, very bad thing…"

Zach stared at the pictures of the five dead men as his world crashed around him. Tobias had killed those men, and Henry had covered it up. Suddenly there wasn't enough air inside. He headed for the door and down the long drive. Scenes from his growing-up years flashed through his mind as he went. Happy times with Henry. All their man-to-man talks about what it meant to be a man of honor and integrity, and the whole time…

Zach reached the end of the drive and bent over, hands braced on his knees, to catch his breath. The pain was excruciating. Worse than when Henry died. At least then he'd still had his memories. Now he had nothing. He straightened and looked down at the badge pinned to his chest. It was all he knew. All he'd ever wanted and now, impossible to keep. He could never look the people of this county in the eyes again once this came out, and it would. Every ugly detail. He reached for the badge to yank it off.

A strong hand clamped down on his shoulder. "That's not the answer and you know it."

"It's the only thing I can do."

Ross narrowed his eyes. "How do you figure that? You've never walked out on an investigation in your life."

Zach shook his head. "Not my investigation, remember? I'm supposed to be le—"

"It's always been your investigation. It's always been ours." Ross' voice was hard with emotion and determination. "You need to finish this, Zach."

Zach turned away, ashamed. "How am I supposed to do that, Ross? How do I live with this? How will anyone trust me again?"

Ross picked up a pebble and chucked it down the drive. "Do you really think you're the first cop in history to come from a family with dirty secrets?" Ross stopped Zach's response with a shake of his head. "I'll tell you how you do this. You do what Henry should have done, best friend or not. You do your job. That's it. That simple. You find those men, and Grace, and you give those families closure. You bring everything out in the open and if the people of this county want you gone after that, you can bet they'll tell you to pack your gear and hit the road." He pinned Zach with an unblinking stare. "Until then, you don't quit, Zach. You don't get to walk away. You feel responsible? Fine, then stay and fix it."

Zach stood staring out across the land Tobias had loved so much. How had it all fallen apart so spectacularly? Ross was right, and he wouldn't quit. He would probably get fired, but until then, he had a kidnapping to solve and five murder cases to close. It was the least he could do for his town before they sent him packing.

He turned on his heel and headed back to the house. Ross paced beside him, thankfully without conversation. There was nothing more to say. He needed action.

Ross followed him back inside the house to the kitchen where Grace's friends waited.

"I know you have to go, Sheriff, but if you haven't done it already, you need to talk to Mrs. Landon."

"Doris? Why?"

"Grace was sure she knew everything, or at least a lot more than she was letting on. She may be the only one who can help us find Grace." Dani's voice was calm and steady but her hands kept up a steady, tapping rhythm on the island.

Zach looked at Ross who nodded. "Worth a try. She left to go to her sister's. I'll get the number and get her back here."

Ross headed out, already on the phone. Zach turned back to Dani and Lucy. "Finding that box was a big help. Thank you."

"What else can we do to help? I can't stand just sitting around," Lucy said.

Zach understood that feeling, but he couldn't have them more involved than they already were. Grace would never forgive him if they got hurt – or taken. He'd never forgive himself.

"What would help me the most is if you would keep going through things in the attic." Zach picked up the two boxes now considered evidence. "And before you wonder, no, it's not busy work. It's important. Grace found one of these boxes and you two found the other. There may be more and we need whatever we can find, especially anything that might tell us where Grace is being held. Will you do it?"

"We'll do it," Dani answered without hesitation, "but would you please keep us in the loop?"

He nodded. "As much as I can, yes." He headed out the door with the boxes under his arm and heaviness in his heart. The clippings were something anyone with an interest in the case might have. Not such a concern. Those pictures though… They were damning in a way he couldn't dismiss. Only someone with intimate knowledge of the crime would have something like that.

Chapter Thirty-Two

With the two boxes from the attic locked in the trunk of his cruiser, Zach took a few minutes to run through a shower and change clothes. His phone rang as he pulled onto the highway and he punched a button to put Ross on speaker phone. "I'm on my way back in, what's up?

"I have Doris Landon in an interview room waiting for you."

"She agreed to come in, just like that?"

"Not exactly. She told me she didn't know anything and she wasn't coming in. I told her I'd get a material witness warrant and bring her back in a cruiser."

"Whatever works. Thanks, man. I'll see you in five."

Zach strode through the station directly to the conference room where Ross waited with Doris Landon. He stepped in and took a seat across from her and next to Ross.

"Doris, thanks for coming."

She glared at Ross. "I wasn't aware I had a choice."

Zach inclined his head, acknowledging that. "Well, thanks for not forcing us to make it official."

She raised an eyebrow but said nothing.

"We're going to record this interview." He glanced over at Ross who started the equipment, then recited the date, time, and the names of those present.

"I'm going to read you your rights and ask if you want an attorney present."

She looked surprised. "Do I need one?"

Zach sighed. "Doris, I can't answer that. I don't want to take advantage of our friendship, but I need information and I need it fast. Grace has been missing for over twenty-four hours."

She pulled herself up, straight as a board, eyes wide with shock. "Grace is missing?"

Zach nodded slowly, trying to read her. "She was taken from the newspaper office and we think Forsythe had something to do with it." He leaned forward to look her in the eye when he continued. "We know about the five missing men, and we know that was Tuck's secret."

The color drained out of her face like someone had pulled a plug.

Anger surged through him and he wanted to pace the room instead of sit at that table. He didn't have time to indulge that desire at the moment. He needed to know everything and he needed to know it now.

"Tell me, Doris. Start at the beginning and tell me everything. Make it quick, and pray that when you're done we find Grace alive."

He should have felt guilty bullying a woman in her seventies, but he didn't. All he felt was anger and sadness that one more person he trusted had lied. He was ready to leave this town and get very far away, but he couldn't leave without Grace.

Doris twisted her fingers together and kept her head down, not saying anything. Zach slammed his hand down on the table, and she jumped and stared at him with huge, frightened eyes.

"Talk."

She nodded and drew in a deep, shuddering breath. Zach forced down a wave of compassion for her. He had no time for that.

"Martin Tucker was the devil," she whispered. "He was mean and conniving and liked to see people suffer. He thought if he wanted something he should have it." She looked up at Zach. "That included people, too, as in other men's wives. He approached several women, wanted to start affairs with them. When they refused, it enraged him and he retaliated."

She stopped and licked her lips. "May I have some water?"

Ross left to get it for her and Zach nodded for her to continue. "How did he retaliate, Doris?"

"He took their husbands."

"The four missing men?"

She nodded. "It was terrible."

Zach felt sick but he had to ask. "Did Tuck know?"

She shook her head vigorously. "No. N-not at first, I swear. He would have stopped it sooner."

Ross returned with her water and she drank it down in one gulp. He left to refill the cup and Zach resisted the urge to reach across the table and shake her. Time was wasting and every minute they delayed was one more that Grace was in danger. He refused to think about her being dead.

"How did he find out, Doris, and when?"

She placed her hands on the table, palms down, and spread her fingers as she took another deep breath. "He saw him. He saw Martin at the bunker. He was carrying one of the men. Tuck followed him down and that's when he saw them. The others that had been there." She stared at Zach with pain-filled eyes and tears flowing down her cheeks. "It broke him. He was never the same after that."

"He knew all this time where those men were?"

She nodded, sadly.

Zach took a few deep breaths to steady himself and asked the question he knew but had to hear officially. A part of him, still in denial, begged for it not to be so. "Did Henry know?"

"Yes."

Zach dropped his forehead to his fists and silently absorbed the body slam.

Doris reached over and gently touched his arm. "I'm sorry, Zach. It was so long ago, before you were born. They decided to never talk about it. To anyone."

Zach raised his head. "Why? Henry was the law in this county? Why would he cover it up, even for Tuck?" He shook his head, still trying to take it in. "Why would he do that to those families?"

"It was such a shameful thing, Zach, can't you see that? Tuck was trying to protect his family. They would have had to leave the county. They would have lost everything. Tuck couldn't let that happen. He couldn't bring those men back, but he made sure it wouldn't happen again."

Zach sucked in a breath. "He killed his own brother, didn't he?"

She sat back with a tiny shrug. "He knew people would think Martin was victim number five. It was better than having them know he was a monster."

"What can you tell me about Martin's son?"

"Do you think he has Grace?"

Zach just stared at her.

Her face and voice hardened. "He's worse than his father ever was. There's something   twisted in him. His father was the devil. He's pure evil."

"Did he know what his father had done?"

She nodded. "He saw him at the bunker and followed him down there once."

"Where are they, Doris? Where did he put them after they were dead?"

She started to cry softly.

"He left them in the bunker?" Zach sat back hard. It all made sense now. "That's why he would never open it for me? Because there were five bodies down there, including his own brother?"

"He thought it was a fitting punishment and he knew no one would ever look there. Justice."

Suddenly he knew, and stood up so fast he sent his chair skidding across the floor. He braced his hands on the table and leaned over her. "That's where he would take Grace, isn't it?"

He headed for the door, Ross on his heels, but stopped when Doris called his name.

"There's one more thing you should know," she said softly.

"Make it quick," Zach snapped.

"He only killed the last one, the one Tuck saw him with. The others, he just left them down there to die."

Zach looked at Ross and shook his head in disbelief. How could this get any worse?

* * *

Dani was waiting for him on the porch when he drove up. He snagged the blueprints for the bunker she'd found for him in Tuck's office and he was off again, after ordering them to stay at the house.

What felt like an eternity later he was up on the bunker with bolt cutters working his way through the lock and the heavy chains, while Ross studied the plans. Zach got the lock off, then pulled at the chains until they came loose and he dropped them on the ground. He jumped down to grab his bulletproof vest and put it on while Ross described the layout of the bunker.

"Here's where we're going in," he said pointing. "The shaft goes down about twenty-five feet to a small room. From there we'll go to a large open space that had three hallways branching off, leading to storage rooms or sleeping quarters."

"This can't be the only way in or out," Zach said. "That lock hasn't been touched for decades."

Ross nodded and pointed again to the blueprints. "Each of these hallways leads to an opening. They come out at various places on the property."

"Send someone to each of those locations and tell them to wait outside. I don't want them going in, but tell them not to let anyone get by them."

Ross nodded, giving orders to the men there with them. They left for their posts, two remaining with Ross and Zach, who had the bunker open and was about to step down into the blackness.

He started down the ladder and made it to the bottom. The barest hint of light shown from around the corner leading him to the large room he'd seen on the blueprints. Corridors led off in three directions but only one was lit. Zach drew his weapon and heard his deputies do the same. They were only a few feet from the hallway when Zach stopped short.

No mistaking that smell. Blood. A lot of it, if the thickness of the odor was any indication.

Please don't let it be Grace.

Zach moved into the hallway and stopped again to take in the scene. The body of Remington Forsythe lay crumpled on the floor, a huge puddle of blood spreading out from what had to have been a fatal head wound. Chunks of broken porcelain littered the floor around him.

Zach peered into the tiny bathroom. Those chunks of porcelain had once been the tank lid. Blood smears covered the sink and the floor. One small, bloody print curved around the door jamb. Someone – Grace? – had steadied herself there. He turned slowly, taking in the entire room. A slug was lodged into the wall across from the door. He stepped out of the bathroom and did a fast search for the gun, but didn't find it.

"We've got a trail," Ross called softly.

Zach ordered one deputy to remain with the body and went after Ross. They followed a trail of bloody footprints down the long hallway. It had to be Grace. The prints were small and spaced close together. He frowned. They were also uneven as if the person staggered as they walked. Twice they saw signs of a fall.

They finally reached the end of the corridor and took the steps to the outside. The hatch lifted easily and Zach let himself believe for a moment that Grace had made her way out and was trying to get home. That hope came crashing down as the deputy keeping watch there held up a syringe with a gloved hand.

"It's recent, boss."

Zach braced on the railing and pushed down his emotions. They weren't going to help anyone right now, least of all, Grace.

"We need to check the other two corridors, and we need to do it quietly."

Ross nodded. "Let's go."

They descended into the bunker again and made their way quickly back to where they'd come in. They chose one of the other hallways and using only their flashlights this time, headed into the darkness to check every nook and cranny.

Please let her be here, and don't let us be too late.

Because if she wasn't here, he was completely out of options, and Grace was out of time.

Chapter Thirty-Three

He's completely insane.

Grace stared at her father's cousin and the wall now illuminated by his flashlight. Martin had turned it into a giant scrapbook of horror. Pictures of the men who had disappeared. Photos of women and children. It looked like every newspaper article ever written about those crimes was included.

Martin taped another picture to the wall and turned to her. "What do you think, cousin? It's almost finished." He held up another photo, yellowed and crinkled around the edges. Two men standing on the porch of an old house.

"Tobias and my father when they were young. Before everything went wrong."

He frowned at Grace. "He killed my father, you know? Tobias. He killed his own brother."

Grace sucked in a breath and shook her head. "I don't believe you. Why would he do that?"

Martin leaned down right in her face. "Because he thought he was so much better than anyone else," he spat out. "He was just like him, though. Just like us. Our family, Grace."

He tossed a key into her lap and then stepped back. "Unlock that and come with me, but don't try anything or you'll regret it," he said as he pulled a Taser from his duffel bag. "Forsythe underestimated you. I won't."

Grace stared at the key, suddenly feeling safer chained to the wall than going anywhere with him.

"I was never a threat to him. Or you."

He snorted out a laugh. "Tobias should have left you alone. It was the nicest thing he ever did for you. Once he sent that letter...well, let's just say he made the wrong people nervous."

Grace closed her eyes as realization swept over her. "You killed them, didn't you? Tobias and Henry?"

He bowed formally. "Very good, cousin."

"Why? You didn't have to do that."

His face hardened like stone. "Because I wanted to. They lived like kings in this county. Upstanding citizens. Pillars of the community. My mother and I had to leave town. We lost everything."

"Tobias would have helped you."

"Why, because we're family?" He shook his head in disgust. "He killed my father!" he shouted. "He left my mother mourning for a man who would never come back. She was never the same after that and I had to watch her grieve herself to death." He stopped for a deep breath and to compose himself. "I made sure he got a good look at me before I killed him. I wanted him to know."

Grace leaned her head back against the wall and closed her eyes, wishing she could shut out the pain. Her heart could not contain the sadness. Her family had inflicted unspeakable pain on this community, then gone on to prosper right in the very heart of all the suffering. How could she even begin to make it right? Assuming she lived to try.

"What day is it?" she asked.

He waved the Taser at her. "Unlock that handcuff. What difference does it make?"

She shrugged. "I'm just curious. It doesn't matter." She tried to reach the lock with the key but fumbled over and over again. She shivered uncontrollably and her vision was blurred, making her squint to focus on the lock. Frustrated, she threw the key at Martin and collapsed against the wall.

"Get up, Grace," he growled. "You're taking the fun out of this."

"I can't. You might as well kill me right now. Just get it over with."

He heaved a huge sigh. "I'm not going to kill you, Grace. I want to show you the rest of the secret." He moved closer. "I'll help you, but no funny business."

He retrieved the key and made quick work of the lock, then grabbed Grace by her arms and yanked her to her feet.

Searing pain shot through her arm and she cried out. She braced against the wall and breathed deeply through waves of nausea. The chill of the cold block wall helped to clear her head.

C'mon, Grace. Get it together and get yourself out of here. You did it once already.

Martin took her by the arm and pulled her toward the door. "Let's go, Grace. One more thing to see and then we'll be done." He kept a grip on her with one hand and held the Taser with the other, but no longer kept it pointed at her.

Not like you're a real threat to him right now. Think!

She stumbled and almost went down, saved only by his grip on her arm. Braced against the wall with her free hand, she moved slowly, ignoring his mutterings. An idea began to take shape in her head, but if she didn't have the strength to pull it off she was dead.

Might as well go out fighting. I'm dead anyway if I don't try.

They went a few more feet and Martin stopped in front of a door set in a niche in the wall. He pulled out a ring of keys, opened the door and stepped in, dragging Grace with him. It was pitch black.

"Are you ready to see the rest of the story, Grace? Meet your great-uncle Martin." With that he flipped a light switch and illuminated the most ghastly thing she could imagine. Five men chained in chairs. Mummified.

Grace waited for the shock to hit but it never did. Maybe she was already there. Maybe the cold and exhaustion had numbed her – literally – to any further trauma. She felt nothing. She turned to Martin who stared at the scene, a small, sick smile on his face. Maybe she wasn't in shock after all, because that smile creeped her out like nothing else, even more than the bodies lined up before her.

As if sensing her watching him, he turned his head slowly toward her. "He didn't kill any of them, really, see? Well, just the last one."

She shook her head slowly. "Why did you show me this?"

"Because, Grace. It's just us now. Just the two of us. No more family left. We have to stick together. We have the money Tobias left you. Part of that should be mine. I kept the secret all these years, don't you see? There should be some reward for that."

He really is insane. It's now or never, Grace.

She took a step then leaned against the wall for support. "I need to sit down, Martin. Can you help me to that chair, please?"

He turned automatically to support her and she fell against him, giving him most of her weight so he would be forced to use both hands to hold her up. She sagged deliberately to give herself another moment, then straightened and pushed him away from her. Surprised, he took a step toward her. She brought up his Taser and fired into his gut.

He screamed.

She screamed. And kept pushing the button to shock him.

He writhed on the floor, but she kept going until his screams turned to moans. She was shaking badly now. Time to get out.

The keys. Where are the keys?

She frantically searched the floor and found them sticking out from under his shoulder. A tiny sob slipped out. She would have to get close to him to get the keys. Too close. She couldn't do it.

Do it right now! Get those keys and get out of here, now!

She held the Taser, ready to hit the button again. He twitched and moaned but made no move toward her. She reached quickly to snatch the keys away but missed both times. Finally, she made herself go slower, slow enough to grab the keys and yank them away. She dropped the Taser and rushed out of the room, slamming the door. It took precious, long moments to find the right key. Something banged against the door and she jumped and screamed again. He was trying to get out. Those loud moans turned to curses on the other side of the door.

She watched, horrified, as four fingers slid out from under the door. "NO!" She stomped hard on those fingers, which disappeared again, as she kept working on the lock. Finally, she heard it click, tried the door and it held. She laughed and cried at the same time. He was trapped. Now all she had to do was find her way out. She dropped the keys and stepped back from the door as someone grabbed her from behind.

Chapter Thirty-Four

She fought like a wildcat, kicking and throwing punches. He would not have believed she could be that strong after everything she'd been through, but adrenaline did amazing things. He tried not to hurt her but in the process, he was taking some pretty solid hits.

"Grace! Grace, it's me. It's Zach. I've got you. You're safe now." He did the only thing he could think of and rolled with her to pin her under him and stop the frantic thrashing. "Grace, look at me, honey. It's me. You're safe now. Look at me."

Glazed eyes stared through him for a heartbreaking moment. He kept murmuring softly to her, willing her to come back to him.

"Zach?" she whispered, finally. "Zach?"

"Yeah. It's me. It's over, Grace. It's over and you're safe."

She started to cry. He sat up, pulled her onto his lap and just held her. Her skin was ice cold. He managed to get his jacket off and around her, pulling it closed to keep that little bit of heat close to her.

Ross and another deputy got the keys and entered the room. He came out a few moments later and confirmed with a single nod, what Zach had expected. He crouched down next to Zach and squeezed Grace's shoulder gently.

"I don't know how you did it, Grace, but I'm impressed." To Zach he said, "Got him with his own Taser. Put him down. Hard."

Zach grinned and tipped his head to see her face. "Did she now?"

"Yep. He's not going anywhere on his own for a while."

Zach tightened his arms around her and kissed her forehead.

"That's my girl."

She lifted a hand to brush the hair out of her face and groaned. "I'm such a mess," she whispered.

"You really are," Zach agreed, which earned him a hiccuped laugh. "Not to worry. I'm good with messes." He rubbed his hand down her arm and she flinched. "Grace."

She shrugged. "It's nothing really. Just a graze."

The burst of fear and fury kicked him hard in the gut. She could have been killed. He rested his forehead against hers and worked to rein in his temper for her sake. She needed calm right now, not his anger.

Her small hand patted his chest, her face tipping up to his. "I'm really okay, Zach. Nothing a hot shower, some chocolate, and a week's worth of sleep won't fix."

He shifted her and got to his feet. "All right, time to get you out of here. Can you stand?"

She nodded and he lifted her gently and steadied her until she got her legs under her. She looked around and frowned. "I have no idea where we are. I hope you dropped some breadcrumbs on the way here."

He chuckled and turned her toward the corridor. The ladder was hard for her and he went up close behind her to be sure she didn't lose her grip and fall. The deputy at the top helped her out and wrapped a blanket around her. Zach walked her to his cruiser, put her in the passenger's seat and crouched down in front of her. She took the bottle of water he offered. He frowned when he had to steady her hand so she could drink. Cold or shock. Probably both.

"Will you be okay here for a minute while I talk to my men?"

She let out a shaky breath and nodded. "I'm good. Thanks for the water."

He nodded. "I'll just be right over there for a few minutes. You'll be able to see me."

Her smile was tired and sad. "Not letting me out of your sight?"

He shook his head solemnly. "Not for a minute."

223

"I'm good with that."

He stepped over to where Ross was directing the scene.

"Where are we with everything?"

Ross leaned against his car, arms crossed over his chest. "As soon as we get Junior out of there we'll seal everything until the state guys get here to work the scene. We have DNA on file for the missing men so making an I.D. shouldn't be too hard. I think." He smirked at Zach. "I'm not really up on mummies."

"Yeah." Zach rested against the car and reached to massage the back of his neck. "What a mess."

"It is," Ross agreed. "But now it's a mess with answers." He glanced over at Zach. "Still want to punch Henry?"

"More than ever." He sighed deeply. "I need to get Grace to the hospital and get her statement. You okay here?"

Ross nodded, watching his men put up crime scene tape and get ready to secure the scene. "We can't do much here for now. I've got men set up to block spectators. We've probably got two hours, tops, before we're dealing with reporters, but we'll handle it."

"Keep 'em out of here, Ross. I'd like to do this as quietly as possible for as long as we can." He looked over at Grace. "For both of us."

"You got it, boss. Go take care of your lady. We've got it covered for now."

* * *

Zach was on the phone with Ross when Dani and Lucy got to the hospital.

"Where is she?"

"How is she?"

Zach clicked off his call and motioned for them to follow. He took them to a private corner of the waiting room so they could sit while he filled them in.

"They're checking her out right now. She's going to be fine. Besides exhaustion, she's got mild hypothermia, dehydration, and some residual effects of whatever drug he gave her. They're giving her fluids and it seems to be clearing her system pretty quickly, so they're not worried. She may need some stitches. They expect her to feel almost perfect once she's rested and had a shower and some hot food."

"Okay, that's good," Lucy said. "Wait, why does she need stitches?"

Zach grimaced. Not something he wanted to tell. "Apparently a weapon was discharged at some point and she—"

"Got shot?!!" They were on their feet like a shot.

Zach stood as well and motioned them all back to their seats. "Grazed. Listen, I'm not trying to minimize what happened, but I want to put it in perspective. The bullet creased her arm and she needs a few stitches to take care of it."

Dani sank back in her seat, pale. "That's bad enough, but I'm sure it could have been worse."

"A lot of things could have been worse." He shook his head, exhaustion settling deep. "Grace is a strong, amazing woman. She's smart and brave and she stayed alive until we could find her. That's what I'm going to focus on."

Dani leaned over and squeezed his arm. "Thank you for finding her. We owe you big time for that."

A door pushed open and a doctor stepped toward them.

"You're here with Grace Tucker?"

"Yes," they answered in unison as they stood.

"I'm Doctor Hanson. Your friend is going to be fine. We've got warming blankets on her and she's got about twenty minutes more on the fluids. She needs rest, food and more fluids. I want to keep her overnight but she's pretty determined to go home. I'll send a prescription for pain medication if she needs it. Someone should be with her for the next day or two, if only to be sure she doesn't overdo it. After that, she can do whatever she feels like."

"We'll be with her, Doctor Hanson, thank you," Dani said. "Can we see her?"

He nodded. "I'll take you back. You can stay with her until she's ready to go if you like. She might like the company."

"Thanks, Doc." Zack turned to Lucy and Dani. "Listen, I need about five minutes with her, then she's yours for the night."

He followed the doctor through the emergency room doors to room five and peeked around the curtain. He stood there for a moment, just taking in the miracle that she was alive. She was battered, bruised, and exhausted, and she looked beautiful to him. He wouldn't blame her if she left and never came back. He pressed a hand to his chest as the thought of that actually hurt. He wasn't sure he'd be staying either. Not sure the choice would be his. Maybe he could give her a reason to stay. Maybe they could give each other a reason.

He stepped in and gently knocked on the partition. She opened her eyes, struggled a bit to focus, then smiled.

"Hey."

"Hey. Did I wake you?"

"No. I was just being lazy for a few minutes between the poking and prodding."

He smiled back. "I think you've earned that." He pulled up a chair and sat back, stretching his legs out under bed. "Dani and Lucy are here. They'll be in soon."

"When did they get here?"

"Early this morning. When they couldn't get you on the phone they knew something was wrong. They came to find out what. Good friends."

A tear trickled down her cheek. "The best."

He couldn't stand it. He leaned over and brushed the tear from her cheek with his thumb. He took her hand, careful of the IV and held it gently. There was so much to say to her and he had no idea where to begin.

She squeezed his hand. "Thank you for coming to get me. I knew you'd come."

He smiled, his heart lightened. "You did?"

She nodded, sleepily. "It's what gave me hope." She drew a deep, shaky breath. "Zach, there's so much I need to tell you about – everything. I wish—"

He stopped her with a gentle finger against her lips. "There's time for all that tomorrow. The state police will need to take an official statement from you. They can do that at the station or at your house, if you prefer. Dani and Lucy will take you home as soon as you're discharged. Tonight your only job is getting clean and fed and rested."

She nodded. "I'll tell them everything I can. Can you be there?"

"Of course, if you want me to be."

"I want to tell you everything, too, but in private before I tell them."

Zach was pretty sure he didn't want to hear most of it, but he would. If Grace lived through it, the least he could do was hear the story and carry the weight of it with her. They both had family issues to deal with.

"Want to do it at home?"

She nodded.

"Okay, I'll set it up for tomorrow about two. That gives you time to sleep in and us time to talk first."

"Okay. Thank you." She rolled her eyes and reached for a tissue. "I'm just a fountain tonight."

"Understandable." He squeezed her hand and stood. "I'd better head out before your friends storm the place. They're anxious to see you."

She smiled. "I'm ready to see them, too."

He leaned over and kissed her gently. "Goodnight, Grace. I'll see you tomorrow."

Chapter Thirty-Five

Grace shifted in the big, overstuffed chair and pulled the afghan tighter around her. She tossed her book on the floor and reached up to click off the light. It was a good night to watch the stars and pray. It was also her first night to be alone and she was relieved and unsettled at the same time, as evidenced by her Bible, the book, and her gun all within arm's reach. She expected to spend this night in the chair and sleep only by accident.

She wasn't the same person she'd been before coming here. She had killed a man. It was self-defense and while there would be no legal repercussions, there were already a boatload of emotional ones. Mark would come back next week and they would talk about how best to help the families affected by everything. After so many years she had no idea what would be helpful, but she was determined to try. She had two million dollars at her disposal. It wouldn't change what had happened or take back the suffering but maybe there was something she could do.

Grace closed her eyes and settled deeper into the chair and her thoughts. After a lifetime of not knowing her family at all it came down to this. What was the point? Why had it been so important to know? What if she'd ignored Tobias' letter and stayed away?

She sighed. Maybe it was her own Queen Esther story. Maybe God put her here just for this. Maybe it was time for the secret to come out before another generation was left to wonder.

Lots of maybes, Grace. Maybe you should just trust that God knows what he's doing and leave it at that.

The phone rang and her whole body jerked, tossing the phone on the floor. She took a steadying breath and leaned over to grab it.

"Hello?"

"Hi, beautiful. What are you getting into tonight?"

The happy in her heart spread all the way to her face. "I'm sitting in the big chair watching the stars. What about you?"

"On the way home finally. Ross is covering the weekend and I've been ordered by my chief deputy to stay away until Monday. Would you mind some company for a few minutes? I have a box of day-old donuts if you need a bribe."

She laughed. "You're welcome, but leave the donuts in the car."

"I was hoping you'd say that. The lights headed down your drive are mine. Do you see me yet?"

"I'll meet you at the door."

By the time she'd unpacked herself from her little nest, he was there. She opened the door and he stepped inside and pulled her to him in a long, tight hug. They stood that way for a long time, drawing comfort from one another.

He sighed. "Just what I needed."

She tipped her head back to study him. "It's been a terrible week, hasn't it?"

"I've had better, but it's over now."

She took his hand and led him back to the study and the big chair. He sat and pulled her down to his lap, then wrapped the afghan around her. She snuggled in, happy and safe.

"I heard the town hall meeting went well."

"They want me to stay, Grace. After everything Henry did, they still want me to stay. I went there prepared to turn in my badge. I wouldn't have blamed them and I wouldn't have fought it but—" He broke off, fighting the emotion of the memory.

Grace shifted to face him. "Zach, they love you and you have served them well. You've suffered with them through all of this and not once did you try to cover anything up or make excuses. How could they not love you for that? You're one of them. This whole county has been hurt by both of our grandfathers but you took responsibility and you brought everything out in the open. You gave those families closure."

"It doesn't change what happened."

"No, but it changes the effects. It lets those families really grieve now so they can heal and move on. In another generation there would be no one left to tell what happened. Maybe that's why this happened now."

"Maybe so."

"Doesn't help much, does it?"

"Not really." He reached up to brush her hair out of her eyes. "Do you think we'll spend the rest of our lives trying to make up for what they did?"

"I don't know. I don't think we ever could, but I'm going to try. I'm meeting with Mark next week to talk about using the money Tobias left to help the families in some way. I have no idea how to do that, but maybe he can help."

"Giving it all away?"

"Probably. I don't need it. The income from the property is fairly substantial and everything is paid off. It doesn't seem right to keep that kind of money, especially since…"

"Yeah. That takes care of you, but what about me? How do I make up for this?"

"You keep being the sheriff they need. Don't minimize the importance of that, Zach, especially now. You've shown them nothing but honor and integrity in a situation that was personally and professionally devastating. You proved yourself to them in a way no one else has, or ever had to, for that matter. They know what this cost you, and you stuck with them every step of the way."

"Henry used poor judgment. Maybe his friendship caused that, maybe it was something else. It was bad, but Zach, don't throw away all the good memories because of this. They're too precious. Part of growing up is realizing that the people we thought were perfect are just regular, flawed human beings after all. It doesn't excuse the bad, but maybe it helps us to extend a little grace to them."

"Is that the counselor talking?"

She laughed softly and rested her head on his shoulder. "Not this time. Just a woman who's making a lot of adjustments of her own."

"Does one of those adjustments involve staying here?"

"I'm thinking about it." She looked around the room and took in the view through the window. "I love this house. Not entirely comfortable here yet, but I'm working on it. I don't know what to do about work."

He picked up a loose strand of her hair and played with it. "You could always open a private practice here. Or, here's another option. The hospital is looking for someone to do grief counseling and stuff." He shrugged. "Just a thought."

She grinned. "I'm good at stuff. Jackson's given me an indefinite leave of absence. I don't think he wants to push me one way or the other and that's nice. It also leaves the decision totally up to me and right now I can't even begin to process all of that."

He rested his cheek on top of her head. "Do you think you could be happy here, Grace?"

She was thoughtful for a moment. "It's a nice town, Zach. It felt comfortable the first day I drove in. For a while all the ugliness got in the way of me seeing the good. Tobias loved it here. Or maybe he just felt tied here because of everything. But he built a good life here. Maybe I could, too."

"Are you up for a no-holds-barred, pull-out-all-the-stops sales pitch? Maybe tomorrow morning over a trash plate?"

"Give it your best shot, Sheriff. Just not before nine."

Epilogue

Six weeks later…

It would take an entire day to clean up. Zach waved at the couple leaving the party and looked around to find Grace. She was saying goodbye to a family with three young children, all of whom had played until they dropped. The cookout had been a wonderful idea, bringing the whole community together as a way to put the tragedies of the past behind them and look forward to the future.

Families were healing and the community had returned to its natural rhythm. The colors of the sunset tonight washed over the land, reminding them of the seasons of life. The good and the bad. Life and death. Hurt and healing.

There was no better setting than Tobias's land, now Grace's. Tables littered the lawn and people had come for food and stayed to catch up and connect. They'd stayed all afternoon. The weather was perfect, warm in the sun, cool now, with a slight breeze as night fell and quiet descended.

Grace made her way to him and they stood together waving as the last of the happy guests left. She turned to drop her head on his chest.

"Ugh. I thought they'd never leave."

Zach laughed out loud. "Not a very gracious hostess, are you? Besides, this was your idea." He took her hand and led her to a hammock tied under two beautiful dogwoods.

"Don't remind me. What was I thinking?"

"You were thinking you'd do something nice for folks around

here who have welcomed you to the community." Zach leaned over and kissed her and the hammock rocked gently. "It was a very nice thing to do, and everyone had a great time."

Grace smiled. "I hope so. There's lots of nice property out here. It needs to be shared."

"It does, and tonight you did it very well." He settled his arms around her more comfortably and rested his cheek on her head, more content than he had been in years, maybe his whole life. "You've done a lot of nice things well, Grace."

She turned her face up to smile at him. "Thanks for all the help. I would have been crazy without you this weekend."

"I'll settle for you being crazy *about* me. That works for me, and in case you didn't notice, it works for just about everyone else around here, too."

She traced his mouth with her finger, then stretched to kiss him. "Works for me too, Sheriff."

"Does that mean you're considering staying on full-time?"

"I could be persuaded."

"I'll be here at nine with a trash plate."

She laughed out loud. "You do say the sweetest things."

Dear Reader...

Thank you so much for reading Grace's story. I hope you were both entertained and inspired by her journey. If you also read my first book, Sacred Ashes, and came back for more, I'm thrilled! If this is the first of my books you've read I welcome you and hope you feel it was time well spent. I'd love to hear from you. I'm on Facebook at facebook.com/authorsherristone, or you can email me at sherristone62@hotmail.com. I would be grateful if you would consider leaving a review on Amazon. I'm busy at work on book three, Lucy's story. In the meantime, if you haven't read book one yet, here's a peek:

The man who killed Dani LaClere's entire family has died in prison after ten years. She expects closure, but her grief is alive and well, and so is her anger at God - and Christians. She plans to deal with it like she always has, by not thinking about it. Easier said than done when she witnesses a murder and becomes the target of a stalker. Her fear escalates as evidence begins to suggest a tie to her family's murder. When a handsome prison chaplain confirms her suspicions, Dani is forced to deal with the pain of her past and a killer she will not see coming.

Find it here on Amazon: http://amzn.to/2krAvYN or type "Sacred Ashes by Sherri Stone" in the search blank.

www.ingramcontent.com/pod-product-compliance
Lightning Source LLC
Chambersburg PA
CBHW071902220626
47052CB00002B/167